S w e e t

Water holds so much power and so much mystery. It is deep enough to keep a thousand secrets, and it is as ethereal as a spirit. It nourishes a barren land back to life as easily as it tears down a mountainside.

With so many facets of this invaluable element to choose from, I was delighted to present this watery theme to five of the most fabulous erotic authors. They have allowed water to inspire them, and they have burst forth with a fountain of tales that ultimately bathe us in imagination and ecstasy.

Water has so much to give that I feel we have barely rippled the surface of this theme, and I am already looking forward to revisiting it again. However, for the meantime, immerse yourself in the pages of Drenched, and do not be concerned if things get more than a little wet!

-Kojo Black

DRENCHED

◆◆◆◆

compiled by

KOJO BLACK

§

SWEETMEATS PRESS

A Sweetmeats Book

First published by Sweetmeats Press 2014

Copyright © Sweetmeats Press 2014

2 4 6 8 10 9 7 5 3 1

ISBN 978-1-909181-72-4

Typeset by Sweetmeats Press
Printed and bound in the UK.

Sweetmeats Press
27 Old Gloucester Street, London, WC1N 3XX, England, U. K.
www.sweetmeatspress.com

Contents

For naughty nixes and seductive sprites

M E L U S I N E

◆◆◆◆

By

J A N I N E   A S H B L E S S

M e l u s i n e

◆ ◆ ◆ ◆

So tonight Martin sits in his rental car, in the country hotel parking lot, watching the stairs to the front door through the rain. It's a filthy wet night. A Friday, of course—what else?

This is how a man breaks.

He's cut the engine and turned off the windshield wipers, in case it attracts attention; and he has the passenger window open for a clearer view. He takes no notice of the seat getting wet on that side; he can afford to pay off the rental company for the extra cleaning. He can afford to buy the car outright, if he likes. Buy it, scrap it, and buy another one with dry upholstery. He's got everything he could reasonably want, money-wise. He's got the perfect life, or that's how it looks; hanging out with celebrities, flying all over the world for business and leisure, two sweet kids, a truly beautiful wife …

Six days a week, anyway.

Not Fridays. Fridays from sunset. Those are … holes in his life. Black spots in the calendar, as if Lucy has taken a magic-marker and blocked in the squares. He can't read what's written beneath. He can't write his own plans. Nothing there but darkness.

And after ten years, that darkness has started to leak out and stain the rest of his life.

Martin sits up straighter as headlights blear the night. Another car, a familiar red BMW, pulls in. Yes: there she is. Just as the private investigator promised—she books into this spa hotel every Friday evening and stays until midday on Saturday. It's two hours' drive from their home in London, and longer if traffic is really bad.

Room 112. She always books the same luxury suite on the corner.

Martin's hands are clammy now. He clenches his fists and then rubs his palms on his trousers as he watches Lucy, wrapped in a long coat, walk to the hotel entrance. She doesn't hurry through the rain; she even lifts her face to let the drops kiss her, as if rain is exactly what she wants tonight.

Lucy always gets what she wants.

She got *him*, after all.

Martin Fiske first met Lucy Doro in the South of France, at the villa of a very wealthy ex-pat client. Martin was there to work on Russ's financial portfolio and partake, at his invitation, in the good things that international television success and Martin's sound financial advice had brought into Russ's life. What Lucy was doing there was never entirely clear to him, but the house was full of friends and assorted hangers-on for Russ's annual birthday bacchanal, and presumably Lucy was a friend of Russ's laid-back wife Angie. Or something.

Martin was sitting with an ice-cold beer on the patio, trying to squeeze in a little work before the afternoon's jaunt down to the coast by prepping a form Russ had to sign. He'd chosen a shaded spot behind the open stairs that led up to the pool terrace, and his eye-line was occasionally broken by feet ascending or descending the broad rustic treads. He glanced up yet again as a door opened at ground level, a woman came out and called a greeting to some other guests, then strolled up the steps— but this time he lost all ability to concentrate on the papers.

From her point of view, the young woman was probably only looking down at wooden treads. From his, he had a direct line of sight as she rose up over him like a vision: hair then shoulders, breasts, waist, hips, legs, feet. Each exquisite part in turn, like some Venus magically emerging from the foamy surf. She was, he thought in awe, golden from top to toe; golden and sleek and smooth, with legs as long as forever. And wearing a very brief dayglo-green bikini, and over that a mini-dress of netted string. That pseudo-dress only emphasised her near-nakedness. It suggested that he shouldn't really be seeing the triangles of bathing suit beneath, or the taut smooth flesh. *Those* should be hidden. Yet there they were—and there he was, looking.

Martin's mouth hung open. The finance form was forgotten. The cheery conversation going on around the patio faded under the thrum of blood in his ears. And then just as suddenly, she was gone, her bare feet stepping lightly overhead.

Someone crashed into the chair at his elbow. Blinking, Martin turned to see Russ grinning broadly at him.

"It's not a bad life, is it mate?" He winked.

"Uh …?" Martin shut his mouth and cleared his throat. "Who was …? I mean, sorry. I was just …"

"Oh, don't apologize. That's the point of all this sun I'm paying for." Russ, his hairy belly toasted brick-red and mounded over a pair of shorts better suited to a younger man, tilted a beer glass conspiratorially in his direction. "Her name's Lucy. Old money, Luxembourg family I believe, likes swimming and photography."

"I wasn't …"

"Well, you should. I've never seen legs like it."

Martin took a sip of his beer.

Ten minutes later—shortly after Russ wandered off again, in fact—Martin was mounting the steps to the pool terrace in pursuit of his vision. He felt embarrassed; he was not the sort of man who followed bikini-babes around. He wasn't, he would have admitted, the sort of man bikini-babes took any notice of, unless they had a daddy complex. But the lure was so strong that it overcame his own self-image as a man of propriety and good sense. He'd like to have claimed it was curiosity; an almost feverish urge to ascertain if she really was as perfect as his brief glimpse had insisted. *No real woman could be that flawless*, he thought. Yet every time he tried to concentrate on his work, those mental pictures rose before his eyes again and overwhelmed him: those incredible long smooth thighs, those exquisite amber breasts cradled in their lycra cups, the near-flat plane of her belly and her lithe waist, and the hypnotic twitch of her hips as she ascended.

He hadn't seen her face properly. She'd worn dark sunglasses, and he'd been too blinded by the body presented below. But he thought she was young. It had been a young body. Far too young for him, he admonished himself; too young for a divorced accountant already turned forty who had found himself playing tourist in a surreal world of sunshine and glamour.

I just want to see. Dear heaven, just let me look one more time. I'll die happy, I swear.

The pool terrace was scattered with people, thank heaven; Martin wouldn't have wanted to be conspicuous. And the pool itself was big enough to justify swimming lengths, which was what that girl, that Lucy, was doing. She swam between the idly splashing knots of pool-users with long smooth strokes. She was gold against the azure pool.

Golden as the sun in the Mediterranean sky above, Martin thought, and staring at her would just as surely make him go blind.

He sat down on a cushioned sun-lounger and opened his file of papers on his thigh, trying to look casual. He could feel the awakened heat in his blood, and the weight of his balls; their speculative clench was an almost unfamiliar sensation. He'd always kept sexual indulgence for the bedroom where it belonged. He'd lived an ordered, proper life and never listened to temptation. That was the way he liked it. Mooning after some strange girl like a hormone-driven teenager was not his style at all.

It wasn't as if he could even see much as she swam. Just the lift of her breasts, perhaps, as she flipped over into backstroke. Just the long taut lines of her torso and the sheen of her flashing thighs. The water hid and distorted everything. It made it hard to judge if his first assessment of her perfection had been correct.

He couldn't leave now.

So he stayed, even when the gong sounded to signal the promised trip down to Russ' fancy new yacht and the champagne-soaked tour around the bay. Everyone else upped sticks and left, even the swimmers who mimed panic and blotted off the water and tumbled themselves into beach-dresses.

One swimmer stayed. She showed no interest in the summons or in anyone else, neither their absence nor their presence. She did a length of front crawl and then a length backstroke and then a silent length underwater, over and over again, absorbed in her own activity, her own body. *Self-sufficient,* Martin thought, glancing up from his papers surreptitiously for the hundredth time, and finding—for the hundredth time—his glance caught on the honey-glaze of her skin for far longer than he'd intended. For longer than it was wise, too, now that everyone else had departed to leave him alone on the poolside. Watching, full of yearning, as she ignored them and him and all the world.

Then she stopped, and drew herself up at the poolside facing him. Her hair was slicked back and darker now, her eyes wide and blinking. Martin cast one last furtive glance and tried to hide his own eyes in the thickets of accountancy. He couldn't help be aware of the rush and the regretful gasp of the water as she jumped and caught herself on straight arms, heaving herself from the pool. He couldn't help seeing, peripherally, as she walked across in front of him to where she'd stashed her towel and discarded clothes. The dayglo-green bikini winked in the corner of his vision as her bottom twinkled past, glittering with water drops. He felt his cock thicken and swell, incorrigible.

The open pages on his lap were a blur. He'd never read another word again, he knew. There was nothing in his head but this Lucy's divine body; half-seen, half-mystery. Wholly bewitching.

Then he heard her light footfalls and saw a blur of tan skin and unnatural green, and he knew she was standing in front of him.

Martin raised his gaze and, with immense effort, looked her in the face.

No sunglasses now. Her eyes weren't blue, as he'd imagined, but olive green, and her long dark lashes were starred by pool-water. Her face … she was just as beautiful as he'd hoped, but he was also relieved to see that she wasn't as young as her body had suggested; her face had the planed look of a woman well out of her first youth, all angles and cheekbones. Except for her lips, which were full and curved in an asymmetric half-smile.

Martin could feel his heart hammering.

She was looking at him. Not just his face, either. She looked him up and down, as if assessing him, and he felt heat charge up to his face and down to his crotch. Did she see a respectable trim man in casual clothes—or a furtive, middle-aged lecher? He knew he couldn't possibly leave now, because if he stood up she'd see he had a hard-on. Quite possibly that was obvious already, but he didn't dare check. Her coolly judging expression made him squirm inside with shame, but it did nothing to quell his surging erection.

Without a word, she lifted her towel and ran it across her wet hair. Tarnished darker by water, a few strands were already turning back to gold—but that wasn't what registered. What mattered to Martin was that in attending to her body right there in front of him, she had somehow granted permission to *look*. So he did.

Dear God.

Was she even human, to look like that? He was a Londoner; he'd married an English girl, he was used to English bodies—pale, fleshy, buttery-soft, sweetly imperfect, and always slightly self-doubting. Not this golden-tan litheness, this confidence, this taut athletic ideal. Lucy had the body of an Olympic gymnast and the assurance of a supermodel. The inner slopes of her delectable breasts—not huge, not small, just utterly perfect, like some impossible lycra-wrapped treasure—were jewelled with water droplets that shivered and ran and begged to be touched, and her waist was so slender that his hands ached to circle it. Those long long legs rose to a tilted pelvic girdle, one hip cocked, the twin ties of her bikini bottom dripping diamonds and tantalisingly vulnerable.

He wanted to lick those water drops. He wanted to touch those breasts and feel their softness and their weight. He wanted to put his hands on those hips and feel the movement of her frame, the way they rolled, as if mere engineering would make her real somehow, make her a thing of earthly possibility. Make her comprehensible to his English sensibilities.

His cheeks burned as he met her gaze again.

Coming to some private decision, this vision flung her towel down across his lap. "Oil me," she commanded.

"Huh?"

"Oil me." Her voice had a husky edge, a slight European accent. She tossed the bottle of sun-oil from her other hand onto the towel and Martin gasped as it smacked right on his burgeoning cock. But the blow did not register as pain; he was beyond that now. He grabbed at the bottle automatically. He was not, however, swift enough to react before Lucy moved in on him, swinging round to present her back and ass and sinking down to straddle his thighs.

He had just enough self control not to swear with shock and delight. He couldn't stop the noise, half earthy grunt and half groan, that escaped his throat, though. And he heard her laugh softly.

Jesus. This can't be real.

She smelled of chlorinated pool water. Most of it was going on the towel, but she was dripping on his papers and his trousers and his shirt. He found he didn't care. He didn't care about anything except the fact that she was sitting astride him, her spread butt-cheeks nestling on his crotch, her strong, slender back presented for his touch. He could see the drops running down the declivity of her spine, right there in front of him, an inch from his raised hands.

This is crazy. Holy hell Martin, don't mess this up! He

couldn't imagine what had he done to deserve this, in this life or any other, but he had no intention of rejecting this gift from the gods. *Carpe diem, you idiot!*

So he flipped the lid of the bottle and squirted sun-oil over her shoulders, though when it came to laying a hand on her he actually held his breath, as if she were some dream bubble who might burst and vanish. But her back was solid and smooth beneath his palm, and not even cool from the pool but warm with her body heat.

He began to stroke the oil across her skin.

"Mmm," she purred, arching her spine.

"Okay?" he stammered.

"Oh yes. Nice." She wriggled under his grasp, thrusting her bum out a little more, with consequences beneath the draped towel that Martin did not dare think about. His brain had locked down to a tiny circle of focus: her body, alive and lithe under his hands, and the slick slide of skin on skin. The concave of her waist, the flare of her hips, the ripe peachy curves of her ass, unconcealed by the little strip of her thong ... Not that he dared touch those. He caressed the oil into her back for as long as he could, dizzy with the scent of sun-lotion.

"Shoulders?" he asked. His mouth was so dry the word sounded woolly.

"Shoulders. Legs. Everywhere," she answered, grabbing the bottle from where it rested at his hip and squirting a line of oil down her thigh.

"Uh. Right." He felt drunk, and clumsy, and unreal. He smoothed his hands down her thighs as far as he could reach toward her knees, leaning into her. Down, and then back up again, smooth as cream—and as he reached her hips she lifted herself a little, raising the perfect heart-shape of her bottom clear of the towel to allow those hands easy access below. "Oh God," he breathed, cupping her butt like he was holding the world in either hand.

"Don't talk."

He nodded frantically, though she couldn't see him. He would have done anything she demanded, so long as he could go on touching that incredible body. Legs, ass, hips—and then, under her guiding hands, round to the front, up from her hips to her waist, over her stomach, back down to her inner thighs, up again, down again. He could hear her sighs of pleasure, feel the heave of her ribs and the press of her groin upon his. His cock was like an iron bar now beneath the damp towel, his hands were thrumming with warmth, and his head was full of the scent of her—chlorine and sun-screen, like the incense of some pagan goddess, making his heart pound. Breathing deeply, he shut his eyes, pouring all his concentration into his hands and his crotch. She writhed back against him, squirming her hips deliciously.

"Up."

"What?" he whispered, his lips in her wet and tangled hair.

"Up here." Pulling down the stretchy fabric of one bra cup, she directed a squirt of oil over her left breast.

Oh God what if someone comes up and sees? flitted through his accountant's mind, half a breath before Martin let out a guttural noise entirely beyond his control and ran his hand in, taking possession of the orb, squeezing and smoothing and stroking. Lucy whimpered, but it was no protest. Her nipple, refusing to be soothed by his caresses, rose up hard and stiff beneath his warm palm, its halo puckered. He didn't wait for an invitation to find its twin; he had both breasts now, both breasts, and this incredible golden nymph was gasping and writhing in his lap, and it was like he had won the lottery and gone to heaven and been crowned king of the universe. And he still couldn't believe it.

"Oh yes." Lucy reached down to the arms of the sun-lounger, grabbed and jerked. That was when the cushioned back collapsed away behind him; a shove of her ass in his midriff sent him off-balance. Instantly his deference reasserted itself; the panicked thought that he'd done something wrong, that he was going to have to pay for his trespass. He felt those fabulous tits slip from his grasp as she rose up, wriggling into a new position and pressing him down. Somehow he found himself flat on his back, with her ass above him dark against the brilliant sky.

Her ass, cheeks parted and thighs bracketing his head, her sex covered only by the narrowest strip of wet day-glo green.

If anyone walks by now—

She put her head down onto the towel and rubbed her face over the mound of his erect cock.

"Christ!" he gasped.

Through the thick fabric, her teeth closed warningly upon his shaft. He nearly came on the spot. Fingers slid into his field of view, pushing aside the isthmus of her bikini bottom, revealing the glistening pink folds of her pussy. They were plump with arousal already—and he'd never seen anything so wonderful, neither in France nor London nor in his private fantasies, not in all the world.

Without consultation she dipped down and pressed her wet slot to his face.

Martin's cry was entirely muffled.

She tasted of chlorine water at first … and then she didn't. Smooth and soft and slick, not a hair on her, tart and musky and hot. When she sat up she nearly smothered him. He didn't care. He didn't need air: he didn't need anything but to lick that pussy and drown in her sex. Nothing else mattered: not the possibility of being witnessed, not the insanity of the situation, not even his own straining cock. He licked her like he was giving worship, and when she came—more swiftly than he wanted, because he could have carried on joyously for hours and hours until darkness fell, or Russ and everyone came back, or he died of happiness—he felt her shake like an earth tremor, grinding her pussy mercilessly into his face as shock after shock pulsed on his tongue.

The moment she was done she slipped away. Her bikini was back demurely in place before he'd blinked the sun and the sweat out of his eyes.

"What's your name?" she asked.

"Martin."

"I like you, Martin. You are very nice." She smiled, and dropped her sunshades over her eyes. All he could see was his own reflection, stretched out helplessly in supplication.

Her bum twinkled merrily from side to side as she strolled away.

That's it then. Over.

Like it could ever have been real.

Wordlessly, he raised himself from his makeshift bed. The girl had got oil on his clothes and his papers, which were mostly crumpled beyond use anyway. Her sex juices were all over his face, the scent sharp in his nostrils. He lifted her towel and buried his face in the soft fabric, breathing sun-oil and pool-water and wild impossibility. Then he gathered up his papers hurriedly.

The towel he kept. He needed to carry it in front of him as he sought out the privacy of his own room, because anyone he met would have laughed to see the stony jut of his erection. Back in his sanctuary, he threw his trousers at the laundry basket and lay back on the bed with the towel draped back over his groin, stroking himself off beneath the soft weight, eyes closed, until the blood roared in his ears and his cum gushed out into the cotton, jet after jet until he felt as if it were draining his heart.

◆ ◆ ◆ ◆

Now Martin gets out of the car and walks swiftly to the hotel, ignoring the puddles that soak his expensive shoes. He has eyes only for his goal, and his heart is so tight inside his chest that each beat seems to squeeze out from within a clenched fist.

He has to know. For ten years he's put up with this ridiculous situation, this charade—but no longer. She has held this thing secret, a part of her life locked away from him, but now he's going to throw open the box.

There's a concierge just within the porch. Perhaps he's supposed to keep the riff-raff out, but he takes one look at Martin's Armani coat and suit, and holds the door wide for him.

Martin goes to the hotel bar, all leather armchairs and dim chandeliers that hardly register in his narrowed vision. He orders a twenty-five year old single malt, and nurses it for half an hour, because he wants to give Lucy time to settle in. Then he pays for a bottle of champagne to be sent up to Room 112 and strolls out, tight-lipped but not cool. His nerves are fizzing with agitation.

He's up the stairs onto the first floor well before the bell-boy arrives with his trolley and ice-bucket, but he sits in one of the plump upholstered occasional chairs in the corridor, pretending to consult his phone screen, until the lift door opens and the young man appears.

"Ah," he says. "Perfect timing," and pulls out his wallet. It's all about confidence. And money. Martin knows what money can do.

The bellboy's lifted hand falters, and the discreet knock he was preparing dies. He accepts the hefty tip with a nod and thanks, and eagerly opens the door with his passkey for the esteemed guest. Martin takes command and wheels the trolley into room 112 himself.

"I want you to take you out to dinner," he told her, the day after their first tryst. Since that encounter she'd shared no more than a few casual words with him, in company, though he thought her smile had a special subtle warmth. He felt it was up to him to take charge of the situation; to show her what he was made of.

"All right," she said, her fabulous green eyes narrowing to almond shapes of amusement. Martin's heart swelled.

"Tonight?"

"Not tonight. It's a Friday—I never date on a

Friday."

The rebuff took him off-guard. "You're, uh, religious?" he blurted—which was possibly the stupidest thing any man trying to tie down a date could *ever* have uttered, he realised a split second after he'd said it.

Her smile broadened a fraction. "No."

"But ..." He cleared his throat, aware that his dominance of the conversation had been punctured. "Not tonight though."

"I always spend Fridays alone."

"Tomorrow?" He hoped he didn't sound as desperate as he felt.

"I'd like that."

He barely held back from whooping.

So on Saturday night he took her out to a tiny one-table restaurant. She wore a long dress in a shimmery pewter-coloured fabric that clung to her body from breast to ankle, and they ate exquisitely simple food on a terrace overlooking vineyards. Their conversation was easy; she seemed keen to draw him out of his habitual accountancy shell, probing delicately at his past, and was interested in everything he had to say. His career was taking off, this sojourn with Russ only one gilt highlight. More nervously, Martin admitted that he had a failed marriage behind him, though no children: the breakup a result of the long hours he worked and his focus on his business. Lucy seemed unphased, to his relief, and sympathetic. When he turned the focus around, she was casually reticent—though he realised that only in retrospect, months later—and acted bored by the prospect of talking about herself. She'd grown up in France and the Low Countries and her family were scattered all over Europe: that was all he found out that evening—or indeed any time after. Too well-off to need real work, the nearest thing she had to a job was some freelance underwater photography projects she'd undertaken, about which she talked with elegant enthusiasm. She liked to swim, as he knew, and read, and travel. She'd "just met" Russ "at the Cannes Festival," and been invited to his house-party. She described herself as "lazy, really," which he found hard to believe.

By the end of the meal he knew himself completely besotted.

After the second glass of dessert wine he kissed her. They kissed for some time, and he put his hand on her thigh. The metallic fabric felt unexpectedly harsh, like tiny scales, and he longed for the smooth skin he knew lay beneath.

"I would like to make love to you," he breathed, his cheek brushing hers.

"Would you now?" There was a tease in her voice. He didn't quite know how to respond.

"I mean ..."

"Yes?"

"What we did the other day ..."

"What about it?"

"It was incredible." Why was this not going the way he'd imagined? "You're ... amazing."

"You think that entitles you to more?"

He withdrew a little, trying to read her expression, but unable to see anything past her faint, challenging smile. "Not *entitles*," he said, though to be completely honest he'd thought of no reason she would refuse him tonight. He'd wined and dined her, after all, and done everything right this time. That was what his ex-wife had told him that women liked—an old-fashioned romantic seduction.

And there was chemistry between them. He was sure of that. The way she laughed, and the way her eyes played over his face, and the warm invitation of her kisses ... he could feel the heat between them. Even now her nipples were pushing up against the fabric of her dress. He brushed one with the back of his finger, and felt the drawing in of her breath.

The vocabulary of romance was dusty on his tongue, but his words sincere. "You're so beautiful ... I've never met anyone like you, Lucy. You make me want crazy things."

She arched a brow, and he quailed as he realised that his pitiful efforts were getting nowhere. Yet her eyes were dark with appetite. He scrabbled for the key that would unlock the cage and release it again.

"I gave you exactly what you were looking for, by

the pool. You want it again, I can tell."

The tip of her tongue peeked into view, sending his heart into overdrive. "What do *you* want, Martin?"

"I want to make love to you tonight."

"What do you *really* want?"

He could scarcely speak. "I want your beautiful body under mine. I want to kiss every inch of you. I want to feel you come again, this time with me inside you."

Lucy's nose wrinkled a little. "Kiss my ass," she said with cold amusement, rising to her feet. For a moment he was staring up, his mouth agape, as she towered over him. Then she stalked away to the terrace balustrade, her high heels clicking on the tiles, and stood in silence with her back turned to him. She wore four-inch heels like daggers, and the cleft of her bare back was an exclamation point of contempt.

Martin was too stunned to react, for a moment. He'd never felt he really understood women, but this was obtuseness taken to another level. His face burned like she'd slapped him. Pushing back his own chair, he rose, swallowing hard.

Where had all this come from so suddenly, he wondered? Had he said something wrong? Or was she deliberately trying to provoke him? Did she want him to march up behind her and turn her with brutish hands and kiss her hard until she broke down into submission, like some 1950s silver screen tussle? Was that what women liked?

The mental picture made him churn inside. His shirt was sticking to his skin. He closed on her, his eyes raking the body that rejected the touch of his hands. Under the slinky dress her bottom was as round and high as a boxing glove brandished in his face.

What do you really want, Martin?

He did what he really wanted. He sank to his knees and lifted his face to the incoming blow. He pressed his face against each firm bum cheek and mouthed her fervently through the thin metallic dress.

He kissed her ass, as ordered.

Lucy sighed.

His hands found the hem just above her ankles. The dress was subtly rough, an old snakeskin; her bare skin was satin-soft beneath. Every inch, all the way up, her dress ruched in his hands. The swell of her ass cheeks at the apex of her thighs made his heart thunder. No narrow strip of cloth veiled her modesty this time; beneath that dress she went without panties.

The discovery made his cock leap.

His lips and tongue brushed those curves, tasting the sweet scent of her skin with each kiss. He nuzzled into the tight cleft and was rewarded when Lucy bent forward over the ivied balustrade stone. Her bottom was like a full moon, filling his sky, and her vulva hung beneath it as if that moon wept a secret tear. With one hand he petitioned her thighs, and she shifted her stance wider to oblige. He tucked the gathered dress over her hip and she even helped him by holding it there. Then he was able to get both hands on her cheeks and spread them to reveal the treasures within. To touch them.

Fingertips. Tongue. She was so exquisitely soft, and this time the scent of her was pure sex.

When he reverently kissed the dusky whorl of her ass she shivered from head to toe.

When he bent and licked her from clit to asshole, she moaned under her breath.

I win, he thought, joyously. *This is how I win.*

It was hard licking her pussy from that angle: his neck muscles protested at craning his head back so far, and his jaw ached. He didn't care. The pain felt like some necessary part of what he offered her; a part of her pleasure, and a part of his. Nor could he be discreet: he ate her noisily, with wet kisses and gusty gasps. She lifted her ass higher and bent over the stone further, thrusting her bottom onto his face, rubbing her pussy up and down with each bounce of her heels. He was slicked with her juices from forehead to chin.

He didn't care if they were seen from the kitchen. He didn't care that the waiter might step in at any moment to clear the glasses. All his need was to eat her: to eat her and to make her come.

Then she did.

He thought he would drown. He thought he would never breathe again, nor have any need to, his mind sliding instead into a place of green waters and long weed, flickering like a fish into the glimmering dark. This woman was an ocean and into her sunless deeps he fell, mile after mile, down to his true home.

She pushed him back at last and stepped away from his reach, but still held her dress up to bare her thighs as she turned to face him. Air hurt his lungs. Lucy's eyes were bright, her cheeks a little flushed, and she was breathing fast. Martin knew his own face was much more of a mess and his own chest was heaving. His lips too felt swollen, burning with her musk.

She had taken him somewhere he'd never been before. A new world.

"Dirty boy," she growled, grinning. She lifted one foot and put the tip of her toe on his chest. Her balance was perfect of course, and the spike of her heel hovered over his heart.

Martin nodded, shaking now. He could see the gold faux-lizardskin straps of her terrifying shoe and the arch of her instep and the pout of her shaven pussy—and there were no words in his lexicon for the ache of his need.

"Let me see your cock," she ordered. The husky element of her voice was very marked.

He obeyed, kneeling there on the tiles of the terrace in his best suit. His length bounced out from his open fly, indignant with neglect, and he felt his cheeks flush deeper as she appraised him.

She laughed. "What's an *accountant* doing with a hard-on like that?" she demanded, letting her toe trail down his torso until her stiletto heel brushed his erection, fencing delicately with the stiff length.

He was too ashamed to answer. Ashamed that his cock was harder than it had been in years.

"Do you want me to hurt you, Martin?" A shift of her foot pressed her sole against the underside of his bare cock, and set the point of her heel against his balls. He could feel the steel tip through his trousers. His heart was hammering so hard that he could barely breathe.

"Please don't," he mouthed.

Her laugh was like bubbles rising through champagne, and then her lips pursed. "Play with it."

"Uh?"

"I want to see you come, dirty boy. Right there. On your knees." Her eyes burned. "In front of me."

His nod was more a convulsion, mirroring the twitch of his cock. As he lifted his hand to the task she withdrew her foot, giving him space to undo buttons and heft his ball-sack out too. The sight seemed to please her.

"That's right. Show me what you're made of."

He did, sitting right back on his heels, cock pointed at the heavens, hands cupping and squeezing.

"Oh yes, jack off for me, Martin. Can you do that?"

He couldn't *not* do that, he realised. The tide was rising in his clenching balls and his cock felt like hot iron under his stroking hand; he wasn't walking out of this place tonight without shooting his load. When, almost absent-mindedly, she pulled down the front of her dress, revealing the golden orbs of her breasts, and began to play one-handed with her stiff brown nipples, he groaned out loud.

"What?" she inquired, archly. "Do you like that? Do you like me, Martin?"

He *worshipped* her. He was trying to keep his strokes slow and smooth, to prolong this moment, to give him more time to feast his eyes, but the taste of her pussy was already on his lips and the roiling in his balls was threatening to spill over into a full-blown eruption.

"You're a goddess," he said thickly. "A fucking goddess." He'd never sworn before, during any sexual encounter. He'd been, up to this moment, a gentleman.

Lucy wet her lips and stepped in until she towered over him. Tenderly she touched his face, breaking the beads of sweat at his temple. Her eyes looked huge, and were green no longer, their colour swallowed in the darkness of her dilated pupils.

"I'm going to come," he grunted, his words all tumbled up.

"Yes," she whispered, straddling him with her long legs and her lethal heels, grabbing the back of his head and moving her mons over his upturned face. "Yes you are."

Her wet pussy engulfed his mouth. He was forced backward on his heels, back and belly and thighs straining, neck tilted at an agonising angle. Only her grip on his head kept him in place. But none of that mattered. He rammed his tongue in among her folds and found her swollen clit and began to suck, his hand pumping now on his cock.

"Now!" she cried, her voice caught up in a rising squeal, and it was impossible to tell if she was referring to herself or to him in that moment, because she was climaxing again as she ground down on his mouth.

And his ejaculation was like a fountain, spurt after spurt jetting into the warm night air, all over—as he found out later—the back of her bare legs and the hem of her rucked dress, spills of cum falling on his white shirt and his best trousers, an irretrievable mess.

This is how a man breaks.

He had knelt to lick off the jizz that had somehow ended up on her heel, just beneath the ankle-strap of those deadly shoes. She didn't even have to order him.

Six months later they were married. It was the very first time she admitted his cock inside her. On their wedding night she pushed him down on the bed and ripped all the buttons off his dress-shirt; she scored his chest with her nails until she left raw streaks, and impaled herself on the stake of his cock and rode him without mercy.

She liked to rough him up, he knew by then. Just a little. Just enough.

It was the happiest moment of his entire life.

Now he's standing inside her hotel room, hands on the champagne trolley, staring around him. His eyes go to the great big double bed first, of course, but it's immaculately made up still.

She's not in the room.

Martin looks around. He's not entirely sure what he expected, to be honest. Lucy and a hairy Latin lover cavorting on the sheets? His private detective has presented sheaves of photos tracing her this far, but no real indication as to what she gets up to inside.

Her case is here, though, flung open to reveal a silk wrap he bought her in Thailand. She always accompanied him on work trips before the children came along, all over the world, and she still does upon occasion. In fact, much of his current success can be laid at her feet: she has a network of social contacts among the higher echelons of society and after their marriage she was keen to advance his career, introducing him to clients he could never have dreamed of.

The air is heavy with the musk of orchids. Lucy loves orchids, and they stand in vases upon every piece of expensive furniture. There's a large antique mirror with a rococo gilt frame on one wall, and he catches sight of his strained face in it. He's a little thinner than on their wedding day, he knows, and his dark hair is flecked silver now, but it suits him. He's better-looking, fitter, more confident, and ten times wealthier. It's all down to her.

She has made him what he is today.

Lucy, it has occurred to him, has not changed *at all*. Not one extra wrinkle, not a stretch-mark, not a single pound of excess weight. After giving birth to Amelie and then Laurent, she'd gone straight back to swimming and her body is the same honed weapon that it was the day he met her.

Ten years, keeping herself lovely.

Obscurely, that troubles him. He's asked her, half-seriously, how it is she stays so young. *Botox darling*, she's answered, *and dermatologists*. But that's too self-deprecating. He keeps a picture of her in his wallet, taken in the week they met, and she looks exactly the same as she does now. Her perfection verges on the uncanny.

And for ten years he's had to take it on trust that that beauty is cultivated for him alone. Because on a Friday, she could be getting up to anything. He's excluded. *Every* Friday night, without fail, without exception. Even when his parents came round to visit. Even when he was presented with a major professional award at a meeting in Switzerland. Even when they were invited to a dinner with the hottest Hollywood star *de jour*. Even when Christmas Day fell on a Saturday, and he had to tell the children their mother was out and wouldn't be home until Saturday afternoon.

It is the single iron-clad condition of their marriage.

"I spend Friday night alone, all night, until Saturday noon. It's me-time, and I give it up for nothing and no one. You can't come, you can't ask me where I go or what I get up to, you can't complain. Do you understand?"

It was the only thing she'd asked of him. Of course, he'd agreed.

And aside from that, she's been the ideal wife. To his initial surprise, outside of the bedroom she showed no sign of the dominance or appetite she displayed—and continues to display—within. She idles through life with serenity and contentment, even complacency. They'd bought a house with a full-sized pool and she swims every day, but aside from that her description of herself as 'lazy' seems not inaccurate. He'll come home at night to find her curled up reading, or pottering about the kitchen. She's always pleased to see him, in her easy, accommodating way. She's perfect, really, for a man in his position—a superb hostess when it comes to entertaining clients, gently charming without being flirtatious, and absolutely unflappable. She adorns his arm on public occasions. She never argues, or panics, or stresses about anything, and she looks with fond amusement upon him when he grows strained. Only in erotic play does the other side of her personality surface— like, he thinks, a docile, sun-warmed snake suddenly waking and rising to strike. Behind bedroom doors she is appetite incarnate: ruthless, shameless and physically dominant. Sometimes he suspects she's holding back for fear she might hurt him.

It's the only time he senses any emotional conflict in her.

He admires her calm. After his previous marriage, he finds a tremendous relief in her phlegmatic ease with life. She has no close friends, no visible family except for him, and no ambition. She watches the world's affairs with disinterest, as if she's seen it all before. But she's happy— and he's been happy, until recently. Only a little bemused, perhaps, by her disengagement.

Even as a mother Lucy seems dispassionate. The hired nannies help take much of the strain out of it, of course, but Lucy's calm never seems threatened. Martin was warned by friends that women go a bit crazy from the hormones while pregnant, and that afterwards they lose all interest in their husbands. Neither happened as far as Lucy was concerned. Birth was swift and easy; both children are pretty and compliant and slept through the night from the very start. They resemble their mother too, to an extent that's almost startling—golden-blond, green-eyed children who play quietly and watch gravely and never give a moment's trouble. When he hears other people complaining about the stresses of parenthood, Martin wonders what the fuss is about and suspects exaggeration.

Sex is always wonderful. He loves it. He loves her.

Yet … on the Friday night one day after giving birth to Amelie, Lucy took herself off to a private nursing suite with the baby and refused entry to anyone else, from Martin to the doctors, for eighteen hours. That had been awkward.

What on earth could she have been getting up to in those circumstances?

He looks at the closed en-suite bathroom door. That's where she is.

As he moves closer he hears the splash of bathwater.

Does it make sense to imagine she's had a barely-concealed lover all these years? What, even when they were honeymooning in the Maldives, and she took a boat out to a private island on the atoll that was no more than a strip of sand and a few palm trees, and had the hotel staff maroon her there overnight? He could remember her walking into their beach-front chalet next day, crusted with sand and sleepy with contentment, just as he was breakfasting.

What sort of secret lover would fly out to the Indian Ocean for a single night's illicit rendezvous, during her honeymoon?

Maybe it isn't one lover: maybe it's a string of them. The thought has occurred to him of course. Perhaps she hires gigolos to satisfy an overwhelming addiction to novelty. Maybe she entertains two, three, a half-dozen ripped young men at a time, of every ethnicity—their enormous cocks like a nest of pythons swarming over her splayed body. Maybe she gobbles greedily at their huge dicks, moaning with pleasure, while other cocks service her pussy and ass. Perhaps it takes several men working in concert to satisfy those near-insatiable holes.

Those fantasy images have plagued Martin's nights alone. Whenever she's away, he has to masturbate to get himself to sleep. His visions have become more extreme over the years: he pictures her whipping men unconscious, or smothering them with her voracious cunt, sucking up the last spouting offerings of their cocks as their heels drum a dying tattoo. He's ashamed of his fantasies, but they make him quake with lust. They make him come so hard he blacks out into sleep before he has time to pull the covers back over his damp and aching body.

Who would guess such a torrid love-life for such an amiable, long-married couple? Who would imagine that the laid-back trophy wife is a virago in bed, or that the dutiful accountant gets his rocks off on being forced and threatened and hurt?

But then, who could picture a mother who refuses to come to her child's hospital bed?

When it happened, Martin rang her. She had a cellphone after all, and this, he figured, overrode any personal agreements between them. She didn't pick up until 3 a.m. on the Saturday morning though, by which time the crisis was almost over.

"It's Amelie," he told her, hoarse with exhaustion. "We're at the hospital. She fell out of the apple tree, onto the wall. Where are you? Why didn't you answer?"

Lucy was evasive. She wanted to know if Amelie was alright. No bones broken? No internal injuries?

"They've done a bunch of scans. X-rays or whatever. They said ... something about skeletal anomalies—but not to do with the fall, some sort of congenital thing. I didn't really get it; that wasn't what I was worrying about. She's got a hairline fracture in her skull and cracked some ribs, but don't panic, nothing like as serious as it should have been. You have to get back here though. She'll need you when she wakes up."

Her family were all resistant to injury, Lucy suggested vaguely. And she'd been told she had unusually flexible joints. And no, she couldn't come back straight away. Tomorrow. "Lucy! For God's sake!"

No. She couldn't come.

"This is your daughter!"

There was no immediate danger. She would not come. Martin would manage fine on his own.

And she'd had her way.

That was nearly three years ago. That had been the turning point: the moment when her solipsistic whim turned from something mysterious and fey, to which his submission was almost an erotic thrill, into … something else. Something darker. 'Me-time' should not be enforced with such ruthlessness, surely, he asked himself? What was it that had such a hold over her that even maternal instinct could not prevail?

There had been arguments after that. Cold, one-sided quarrels of few words but many black looks. Martin did not know how to shout, or to bully. His tactic with his ex-wife had always been to retreat before her flaring frustration and withdraw into his own head, lips pressed together in silence. Now he found himself facing the same strategy. Lucy only flicked her golden hair over her shoulder and looked at him, long and sorrowfully, and when pressed to the limit said, "You promised."

Yes, he'd promised. And he's a man who reads the small print and accepts what he's signed up for—so in the end he'd stopped reproaching her. But the resentment and the fear did not go away, only churned and curdled inside the pressure cooker of his ribcage, until he felt it leaking into every part of his life.

And now he's standing at the door to her bathroom, in the luxury hotel bedroom, with his hand on the porcelain knob. He can hear the slop of water beyond the boards, and the hiss of a running tap. He knows she's in there.

Maybe she's alone. Maybe not.

He knows he should not be here. He said he'd respect her privacy.

He promised.

The ceramic is slippery under his fingers as he turns it. The bathroom is lit by candles, reflecting off mirrors, and for a moment he can't make out much more than the great sunken bath in the centre of the floor. It's the size of a small pool and she's completely submerged beneath the darkly glinting water. It takes a moment for her head to rise above the surface, and in that moment he can feel his heart banging against his breastbone like a trapped animal trying to flee.

She opens her eyes and blinks away the water. He hefts the bottle of champagne.

"Happy anniversary, darling," he says.

As she tilts her face up to him, the candlelight catches strangely in her dilated pupils, and for a moment he sees blank disks of cold fire. One glistening shoulder rises from the pool and her lips part. Between them there is darkness. He hears the hiss of her breath.

"Ten years," she says, and she sounds calm but he can hear something huge pressing up behind those words, as if they are the bars of a wholly inadequate cage. "I've been waiting. I've wondered every single time if this is it, if this is the week."

"Sorry to have kept you on tenterhooks, darling.

It must have been quite a trial for you." He swings an open palm to indicate the mirrors and the candles and the polished marble. There's a quiver in his throat that he hopes she can't hear. "Well, where is he?"

"Who?"

"The guy. The girl. Whoever it is that you come to meet."

She tilts her head, leaning forward a little. Her shoulders catch the light and gleam like fire. "I come here to be alone."

"That's a hell of a lot of expensive baths, Lucy. What's it about? All this?" His voice rises. "I've had enough. I want to know."

She smiles, but there's no warmth in it. "I suppose ten years isn't so bad, Martin. Others have done worse."

"Others?" He steps forward, feeling the sweat running down the insides of his thighs. He's broken the only taboo, and now he realises how much he's afraid of her wrath.

Fear has given him a most inappropriate and tumescent erection.

"Well, you're not my first husband, you know."

He didn't know. How could he, when she never talks about her past? When she never reveals *anything* about where she comes from? He wants to be outraged, but he's already overflowing with turmoil and there just isn't room for more. He wants to stare her in the eye, but his gaze can't help falling to where the water-line laps about the curve of her breasts, just barely concealing the twin points of her nipples. The hint of a dark areola nudges the surface. That almost-revelation, the tease of the near glimpse, itches at him.

"How long did the last one put up with this crap?" he asks.

Lucy curls her lip in a laugh that is all hiss and no humour. "Eighteen months. But the one before that, twenty-two years."

Impossible. His cock is rubbing uncomfortably against the fabric of his pants and he wants to adjust it, but he doesn't dare touch himself. "I'm so sorry I don't have that much patience," he growls.

"I'm sorry too." Lucy arches her back and his cock twitches in gratification as her breasts break the veil of the water at last, nipples as stiffly erect as if it's ice she's been bathing in, droplets plashing from their swollen points. "I thought we had an understanding, Martin."

It doesn't need the beckon of her lifted hand to bring him forward; he's already moving closer. He can't help it. Right to the edge of the bath, looking down at her. Her skin gleams, lacquered by water and candlelight, and her nipples stare back up at him like bold dark eyes. She's exquisite, and even after all these years she makes him ache. "I never understood," he confesses. "What the hell's going on here?"

She rises up in the bath before him, slowly, and the water sighs like it misses her. Up and up and up, until her face is level with his. Breasts and waist and hips and … *He doesn't understand.* He looks for the juncture of her legs, the familiar pout of her pubic mound, but he doesn't see it and he can't understand what he's looking at. No velvety cloven pussy with its promise of concealed delights, but a vertical cloacal slit. No thighs, no long long legs— just flesh, more flesh, a muscular unbifurcated column disappearing into the water where her knees should be. No joints. A tail. *She has a tail instead of legs.* She's standing up on a thick pale length like a snake's—no, more like a lamprey's or a hagfish's—and there must be coils and coils of it still underwater to support her upper body that way. He can see diaphanous fins whose webs of translucent skin glow like stained glass with the candlelight behind them, and the faint shimmery pattern on that skin that's not truly scales but hints at it, and his mind is full of words like *sea serpent* and *wyrm* and his mouth is open and he's forgotten how to breathe—but the air is going out of his deflating chest with a noise like he's never made before in his life.

"Do you understand now?" she murmurs, laying a hand on his chest and sliding her fingers between his shirt buttons.

He can't answer. Yes, he understands, because it makes sense at long last: why she never talks about where she comes from; why he's never met her family; why she never ages. But the words bunch inside his throat and refuse to come out, as if they think they will be safe there. He can only look down, wide-eyed, at the pout of her breasts and the play of her wet hand on his shirt, and at the great inhuman mass below. So he sees the other end of her tail as it comes snaking out of the bath and slithers toward him, muscling up between his calves and wrapping about his thighs in a figure-eight. The golden eel-flesh feels surprisingly warm despite its slickness, and almost soft— until the muscles beneath contract. He doesn't try to fight as she pins and binds him; he knows already that she'll be far too strong for that.

So it doesn't really surprise him when she digs her long nails into the cloth over his crotch and tears through the fabric like it's no tougher than a paper towel. She shreds his trousers until his groin is laid bare; he feels the cool air but he doesn't dare look. Those nails must be sharp as razors. He meets her eyes instead, searching frantically for something human beyond the vertical ophidian slits that her pupils have now narrowed to.

"It's a pity," she murmurs, her lips almost brushing his. Her breasts are making damp prints on his shirt. "I liked you, Martin."

The champagne bottle is heavy in his hand, and threatening to slip from his numb fingers. It's heavy enough to be a weapon—if only he could wield it decisively. If he could pull away enough to get a good hard swing, instead of pressing up like this against her. If he could stop thinking about the way his balls are tight with fear and his cock taut to the point of aching as it butts and rubs against her through the rents in his clothes, no longer constrained.

"I liked you very much," she concludes, bearing him over, off his feet altogether now, flat on his back with his legs tangled in her coils. Water washes over the bathroom tiles, soaking him as his shoulders hit the floor. Somehow he's kept the bottle aloft, his instinct recoiling from smashing the glass. Lucy wrests it effortlessly from his grip with one hand, and as he lies beneath her she snaps the green glass neck with a press of her thumb.

He's appalled by her strength.

Champagne gushes out and falls, a frothy magma.

"Have a drink, Martin," she urges, tilting the bottle over him. Champagne foam slops on his shirt and throat and face. "One last drink to remember me by." It's glugging on his face, fizzing up his nose, filling his mouth. He twists his face away, trying to catch his breath as she pours it over his lips, snorting and gasping the golden liquid out of his airway. "One last time, Martin," she repeats, slithering over him. She has no hips any more, no pelvic girdle, but she's pressed against him where her hips used to be, and his cock is so stiff between them that even her firm flesh must yield to its jut. All of a sudden that narrow slit of hers finds itself in conjunction with the swollen bell-end of his erect cock. Blindly, frantically, the two push together. "One last time!" she gasps as she engulfs him.

She's hot and tight and slithery-wet inside, and she *sucks* on him.

"Oh!" Martin gasps, choking on the falling champagne, his hips bucking. It's never been like this before, not even in their finest moments. Lucy looms over him like a falling angel, her breasts shuddering as he thrusts up into her; mouth open like she's going to swallow him whole. She's pinning him and half-drowning him— he's beside himself with terror—and it is just *perfect*.

Then the champagne runs out. The last splash glugs out on his writhing lips and then she tosses the empty bottle aside. He hears it smash against the marble. For a moment they both go still, breathing hard. Martin blinks stinging eyes and looks up in supplication into hers. If this were any other sexual encounter between them, this would be the moment she would slap his face.

Oh, how nervously he'd begged her—flushed with his shame and need—to slap his face, that first time.

But this is no ordinary bout of sex play.

That's the moment he feels it: the narrow tip of her serpentine tail, inveigling its way between his ass-cheeks. It's smooth as silk, a little slick, and far too strong to resist.

With a despairing cry Martin arches and tries to thrash his way free, but he's locked in a baroque tangle of limb and tail, his legs held open and his butt-cleft defenceless. When he tries to push at her shoulders she captures his wrists and pins them to the tiles, pressing down with all the weight of her torso, and he feels her wet clench about his cock, like a fist pulling him back into place.

"Oh Martin," she purrs, and it's the growl of a monster.

He stops struggling, locked in place. He doesn't dare fight it.

The invasion of his ass doesn't even hurt: that's the shameful thing. She slides into him like she belongs there, like he's a sheath made for her, like she owns him. It feels like what he's been waiting for his whole life, and though he never knew that, somehow his body did; his ass surrenders to her without resistance, no matter how the muscles of his legs and arms strain. Nerve-endings he's never guessed at spark with pleasure as she slides in and out, easing his clench, deep and then deeper. Lightning flickers up through his body and flashes behind his eyes. Now he's making bestial noises, and calling on God—but God isn't there, can't be there, not the God of mercy and truth and purity. Only the *magna mater*, dark and golden-gleaming, overwhelming him, possessing him inside and out, filling his ass and milking his cock and stooping low over his face to bite his lips bloody.

"One ... more ... child ..." she groans, her voice trembling, her eyes hugely dilated. Her lithe not-hips dance, driving her slippery cunt up and down on his shaft even as her tail pumps in his ass, touching places that have never been touched before. And Martin knows he is lost.

There.

Oh God yes.

Swept away. Gold and black, flame and darkness, like a great flood-tide. He pours out his pale gush, and for a moment his own light burns like phosphorus in her depths. She is the whirlpool Charybdis; she is Tethys; she is the Ocean and he is drowning in her.

And he wants nothing else.

But when he surfaces, long hours later, cast back up on the shores of consciousness, she is propped up on her arms looking down on him, and there is no goddess or serpent in her eyes. Just, for a moment, the Lucy he thought he knew.

She looks pensive.

"I should kill you," she says softly. "That's what I'm supposed to do. To keep the secret."

Martin runs the dry tip of his tongue across his swollen lips, tasting salt and blood.

"But," she murmurs, "the children will need their father. Goodbye, Martin."

"Don't go," he says. "Please!"

For a moment she holds his gaze, regret naked in her face.

Then candlelight dances only on an empty bath,

on smashed bottle glass, on slick tiles. He feels the hot hard tears gather in his chest and writhe their way up toward his throat.

This is how a man breaks.

The fairy Melusina, also, who married Guy de Lusignan, Count of Poictou, under condition that he should never attempt to intrude upon her privacy, was of this latter class. She bore the count many children, and erected for him a magnificent castle by her magical art. Their harmony was uninterrupted until the prying husband broke the conditions of their union, by concealing himself to behold his wife make use of her enchanted bath. Hardly had Melusina discovered the indiscreet intruder, than, transforming herself into a dragon, she departed with a loud yell of lamentation, and was never again visible to mortal eyes; although, even in the days of Brantome, she was supposed to be the protectress of her descendants.

- Sir Walter Scott: *Minstrelsy of the Scottish Border*

THE POOL PARTY

◆◆◆◆

By

PRIMULA BOND

The Pool Party

◆◆◆◆

"I'm glad we made the effort to get up so early," remarks Kara, setting up her easel. The first lemony fingers of the morning trace the craggy walls of Roquebrune castle. "It's so quiet! No tourists yet. No traffic. And look at the sea down there! It's like wrinkled silk."

"Loving your enthusiasm, honey, but we're only catching the sunrise because those fucking mice kept us awake all night." Suki yawns, pouring two black coffees from the cracked thermos flask they found at the back of a dusty cupboard. "And I'll bet that when we stagger back to the creaky old hovel that there won't be any water for a shower."

"You're making me feel really guilty now for dragging you here. The plan was to waft about on the Cote d'Azur, following in the footsteps of Picasso and Matisse and their merry men, but it's not exactly paradise, is it?" In the few minutes it has taken Kara to dip the soft sable of her paint brush into her palette to mix powder blue and white, the dome of sky has been washed with a starker, harder blue. She flattens her brush against the canvas and makes the first sweep. "There isn't even any local talent we can get our mitts on!"

The girls both breathe deeply. You can get high on those paint fumes.

"Don't remind me. All this sun and sleeplessness is making me horrifically horny!" Suki watches a hang glider launching from the cliffs above their heads. It wheels and arcs through the air like a green and orange striped bird of prey. "And you know how grumpy I get when I go without!"

Kara laughs. "You'll be dragging that old geezer who gives you free *pastis* in the village bar back to bed for a good hard ride if we're not careful. Or maybe we should just cut short this vacation and go home."

"You're normally the sensible one, K. Not a quitter." Suki taps her sketch pad against her chin. The hang glider hovers over a strip of beach far below. "We've only been here for three days!"

Kara glances up. Her friend's limbs already glow with a honey-hued tan and the strengthening sun is turning her fair hair to buttery curls of gold. She rubs at her still-pale skin and tries to ignore a sudden twist of jealousy.

"Let's go into Nice tonight and have a few drinks in the old town. We'll make a decision tomorrow."

The hang glider lands silently on the sand.

It's early afternoon when the rental car bumps reluctantly back up the rutted lane overhung with ivy and vines. The pink cottage looked so quaint when they first arrived here, so brimful of promise and adventure, but in the glaring sunshine it just looks scruffy and there's an eerier silence than normal, broken only by the cooing of a pigeon which has made its nest in one of the bedrooms.

"The electricity's gone again! The milk's gone off, and even the wine and beer are warm!" Suki snatches out a bottle of mineral water and slams shut the fridge, sending a family of huge black spiders scuttling across the floor. "I'm going to find a signal and phone the bloody airline to change our tickets!"

Kara is nowhere to be seen. Suki marches to the end of the garden, ignoring the terraced vista of vineyards and tiny villages unfolding beneath her. She holds her arm up and waggles her phone desperately at the sky. Nada. She's opening her mouth to swear blue murder when there's a sudden flurry of leaves and twigs and wings over the other side of the riot of bougainvillea hiding them from the world like a couple of sleeping beauties. Two bright blue kingfishers swoop out of the garden next door and up into the sky.

"Is that you breaking and entering, Kara? What are you thinking!?"

There's no answer. Suki clambers up on the old stone wall. The heat sings in her ears. Her tongue feels thick and dry, sticking to the roof of her mouth.

She doesn't stop to query what made the birds startle like that. All she can think is that if there are kingfishers over there, there must be water.

Through the tangle of greenery she sees an expanse of velvety lawn. Her gaze is led past marble statues of naked goddesses, past sculpted topiary in vast terracotta pots, and lands on the sapphire glitter of a swimming pool. It's so bright and tempting she can't hold back. Within minutes she is pushing through the branches, ignoring the twigs scratching at her skin, and running up through the grounds. She's vaguely aware of the white wedding cake facade of her neighbours' grand villa, but she'll deal with any trouble later. Right now she's so hot she just dives, fully clothed, into the cool water.

She reaches the mosaic tiled floor of the pool, lies there for a moment, then turns and swims swiftly to the other end, her body merging fluidly with the watery element, lungs stretching to bursting point, the sky wavering above her, no sound, only her limbs pushing aside the weight of water.

As she spreads herself like a starfish and floats up to the surface, she glances around. The French doors of the villa are all closed. They're rectangles of enticing darkness, inviting her to explore the forbidden interior.

Maybe it's time she made herself scarce.

She climbs out, but she can't bring herself to leave.

Next door there is one broken sunbed and rough garden furniture bristling with splinters. Here there are luxurious, white, squashy loungers to recline on. And big white umbrellas. And polished teak tables.

Suki is torn between running back to find Kara, and staying right here to taste the joys of this secret garden, like Goldilocks. Goldilocks wins.

She peels off her dress and sprawls out on one of the loungers, barely covered by her soaking pair of panties. One leg and one arm are dipped into the water, the other arm rests across her stomach. A trickle of moisture runs from under her hair down the side of her face.

Idly, and with her eyes still shut, Suki lets the sun sink into her skin. Her fingertips trail over her breasts. Her nail catches on one nipple. It tingles into a tip, the hard nipple trapped between her fingers like a bud. A shudder runs through her. She can't help it. Her other hand wanders down between her legs and peels aside the wet fabric.

Suki feels like a lizard, motionless. The heat is welding her to the cushions.

A shadow flits across her closed eyelids and away. Her nostrils quiver. There's the smell of another person's sweat somewhere nearby. Sweet, but strong. Her fingers cease their wandering.

"Kara? Is that you? Come and see what I've found! How about this place for a proper paradise?"

Suki opens her eyes, peering through the fringe of

eyelashes, but instead of her friend's white, coltish legs she sees a muscular brown pair standing at the deep end.

"*Bonjour, mademoiselle.*"

A bubble of fright and excitement blocks Suki's throat as the deep French accent growls across the space between them. Great. Now she's been caught trespassing. But the scary guy doesn't look like he's about to throw her out—not just yet, anyway—because he's currently holding a huge droplet-beaded crystal jug of some kind of cordial, swirled with oranges and jangling with ice. From where he's standing he can definitely see her hand in mid-stroke upon her pussy.

She bites her pouting lower lip in a shy little girl gesture. If she gives him a treat, maybe he'll give her a drink. And if she gives him a really *special* treat, maybe he won't punish her for breaking in.

Intoxicated with sunshine and possible danger, she opens her legs a little wider, lets her finger drift even more obviously up the glistening pink crack. Her finger is the only part of her that is moving. All she can see is a silhouette, black against the dazzling sunshine. The figure doesn't move. He's wearing sunglasses, but she knows his eyes will be fixed on what she's doing because her finger is tickling and teasing, dipping inside, pulling out again. As she pushes in, harder this time, she runs the palm of her other hand over her exposed nipples and as they harden with pleasure her spine arches instinctively, displaying her to her audience.

"*Bonjour.* I'm staying in the cottage next door, but I know I'm trespassing. Very naughty. Je suis tres mechante," she breathes, bucking gently against her own finger. "So you better punish me, monsieur."

The man hesitates, takes a barefoot step towards her, then stops again. Suki pulls her finger out of herself, holds it up in the air to show him the juices. Then she licks it. That's done the trick, because now he's kneeling down at the foot of her cushion. He puts the jug down on the paving stones. She squints through her eyelashes. His erection is shoving against his faded shorts. Up close he's much younger than she thought. He's hunky but hairless. Watchful, yet wary.

Suki sits up and leans forward, runs her tongue over her lips. She lifts his sunglasses off his nose. Dark chocolate eyes in a handsome, tanned face stare back at her. Long, thick eyelashes. White teeth barely out of braces. Christ. He can't be more than seventeen.

Next, she dips the silver ladle into the jug of sangria or whatever he's brought and takes a greedy gulp.

"Where is your boss?" she asks, leaning back and running her foot up his chest. "Is he going to come out of the house any minute and catch me? Maybe call the police?"

The hunky gardener catches her foot and pushes it back down. "My boss?"

"*Le patron. Le maitre de la maison.*" She nods towards the grand villa. The only sign of life is the corner of a white curtain blowing from an upstairs window. "Am I in trouble?"

He shakes his head. "They are away in Paris. I am alone here."

"*Alors, viens,*" she whispers as a deadly daring takes over. She grabs him and pulls him closer. "Embrasses-moi."

The boy allows her to touch him as he studies her, his eyes roaming hungrily over her body. "You invite me to kiss you?"

Suki lays back. She's never come on to anyone younger than herself before. Or anyone French, for that matter. But hey. They're two strangers in a hot garden. This is a one-off. It's going to be fun.

"Ha! So your English ain't bad! *Oui.* I'm inviting you to kiss me and maybe a whole lot more than that. Let's see. How do you French say it when you want to get down and dirty? Baise-moi."

"I understand it perfectly." The gardener is grinning openly now. "You want me … to fuck you?"

The knowledge that they are out in the open and that Kara might discover them at any moment only turns her on more. The sun is so hot she feels as if she's melting. She giggles and tips herself towards him. Her boy doesn't need to be told twice. He rips her panties off and guides two stout fingers into her ready, wet pussy. She gasps and tries to rock against his hand, desperate to relieve the building, burning pressure. But he, more confident now, or so aroused he just can't resist, pushes her down roughly.

She flings her arms over her head in surrender and arches her body at him. He may be trying on the masterful act for size, but he's biting down on his lip, vainly trying to hide his lust. He may not be a virgin, but she can tell he's never been offered it on a plate like this before. A tremor runs through her as his fingers pause inside. She wants him to think of her as his first. She wants him to remember this encounter for the rest of his life.

Just then she hears Kara calling, far away in the garden of their tumbledown cottage.

"Shit, she'll be wondering where I am!" Suki hisses, lifting her legs and wrapping them round the boy's hips. "You gotta hurry."

The boy shakes his head, his fingers sliding out of the wetness and wandering over her body.

"Doucement."

He wants to do this sweet and slow, and normally that would be just fine with her, but he hasn't understood. Her best friend is about to walk in on them. The boy just grins and starts to fondle the ripe breasts she's offering him. He leans down and bites hard on one dark nipple, sucking it and sending shocks of desire shivering down to her cunt. Then he plays with the other one, squeezing them together so that the red nipples are standing side by side, burning for attention.

Suki forgets about her poor friend, or the fierce master of the house, whoever he is. She decides there's no rush and pushes herself against the boy's eager face, grabbing his hair and angling her nipples brazenly into his mouth, feeling them scraping them against his teeth, begging him to suck her.

"Suki, you're freaking me out now!" yells Kara from the other side of the hedge, unmistakable anxiety ringing in her voice. "Stop messing around and answer me!"

Suki couldn't call back even if she wanted to. She can only grunt and moan now. Her moist pussy is stuck to the boy's shorts, the tiny curls caught on the fabric, tugging the tender skin before letting go. He's hurting her now, biting and nibbling as her nipples stretch taut, pleasure mingling with pain. Her hips start to gyrate, answering the messages sent down from her tits.

She takes the waistband of his shorts and starts to pull them down over his smooth, warm buttocks. "You gotta fuck me! Vite!"

The boy stops sucking her nipples, leaving them burning and sore. He kicks off the shorts, and there's his young cock, hot, huge and hard. Her whole body shudders, her cunt clenching impatiently to have that inside her. How the hell has she gone this long without sex? Kara is still calling, her voice undeniably getting closer, but Suki doesn't care any more, and nor does the boy.

She grabs hold of his cock and rubs it up against her, letting him feel the softness, the wetness. Her cunt squeezes hungrily for him. He groans and buries his face in her neck, biting at her sweaty skin as he falls heavily on top of her.

Suki takes over, as she knew she would. She eases the tip of him just inside her and then grinds into him, driving him into her, digging her nails into his buttocks. He comes to life and grips her hips, going straight into gear, matching her rhythm and pushing his cock further and further up. He's so big. The biggest she's ever had. And the hardest. Oh God, she could get a taste for these young guys!

He's swearing under his breath, slamming at her, faster and faster. If she's not careful he'll come too soon, they're already humping so furiously. She grips him with her thighs, thrusting her hips against him, cramming him in, grinding down so that he fills her with all those solid inches of rock-hard, thrusting cock and the orgasm gathers crazily and quickly, ready to and break any minute.

She knows Kara's right in the garden now. She can hear her friend's bare feet swishing on the dry grass. But it's too late now. She's coming closer. Seeing the two of them fucking like this will shock her to the core, but they can't stop.

And they don't. Not until the climax explodes and they collapse in a tangle, shuddering and sweaty, beside someone's else's swimming pool.

Kara clears her throat.

"I take it you're having such a good time now that you won't be packing your bags any time soon?"

Suki rolls over and grins.

"That's right, sister. Forget going home," she giggles, feebly trying to cover her hot, wet body with a sliver of towel while the boy draws up his knees in an effort to hide his still-hard cock. "I reckon since there's no one here to stop us, we should play free and easy with this lovely pool. And this lovely pool boy! What was your name, by the way?"

The boy wriggles into his shorts and stands up shakily.

"*Je suis* Francois. And I'm not the pool boy. I—"

Suki aims a kick at his ankle. "The gardener. Butler. Whatever. Can you find us a beer, Francois?"

"God, Lady of the Manor, or what! How do you get them eating out of your hand like that?" Kara sighs as the boy puts his sunglasses on again and slopes up to the house. She sits down at the far end of the pool, dangling her feet into the cool water and nearly coming on the spot with the pleasure of cold water on her over-heated skin.

"It doesn't take much, K, if only you'd try it. Just

one horny male, a tight, wet pussy and a bit of attitude."
Suki slides back into the pool like an otter. "Come on,
loosen up. I'll share my gorgeous young stud with you,
if you like. How about a threesome? Make this a holiday
you'll never forget."

"I'll pass, thanks. Don't really like you in *that* way."
Kara grins and sweeps a wave of glittering water over her
friend as Suki cackles with laughter. "And anyway, what
about the owners?"

"What, you think you'd like them in *that* way?"

"I mean, when did your stud say they were coming
back?"

Suki turns on her back and kicks back up to where
Kara is sitting. "He didn't. I didn't ask. We're not doing
any harm, Kara. Just having fun. Come on in. The water's
lovely."

Kara hesitates, then pulls her shorts and tee shirt
off and rolls into the blue water.

"So long as you promise to come and paint with
me in the mornings like we agreed, and you don't sleep
over, or break or steal anything, I guess you can do what
you like."

Two days later, and Suki is in full bitch-on-heat
mode. She won't be prized away from Francois. As soon
as the girls have completed their dawn painting sessions in
the mountains, or on a cobbled village square, or near the

sea, Suki rattles the old jalopy back to the cottage and then tears off next door to find Fraoncois to get him between her legs.

And what Kara likes, she discovers, is being alone. Well, as far as you can be when you're never more than a few yards away from the moans and giggles of your best friend and her new toy boy. Suki and Francois started off making out in the shade of the majestic palm trees guarding the grounds, but today, thank god, they have ventured into the house. Corrupting the master bedroom, no doubt.

She won't watch. She saw them that first time and was shocked at how arousing it was. Suki's golden hair spreading like a lake beneath the dark body bent intently over her. Their limbs melting and entwining, the boy's muscles flexing, his buttocks tightening and thrusting, the illusion that such rough movement must hurt, yet knowing it was giving her friend the most exquisite pleasure ...

She enters the garden the official way, through the side gate, and passes a neatly stacked hang glider beside the garage. As soon as she sees the glittering pool she breaks into a run in an effort to shake off this new restlessness. Pausing only to strip, she dives in.

Today she is challenging herself to swim as many lengths as possible underwater so she can stop thinking. What's wrong with her? Why doesn't she want a piece of Francois? She can see he's beautifully formed and extremely well hung. She's even sketched him lying by the pool taking a rare breather before Suki dragged him off again.

But when he's not fucking her friend, when it's just him on his own, there's not a flicker of real desire. She's not attracted to Suki, but she's not attracted to Francois, either. There's no tightening of the stomach or racing of the heart, even while she's staring at Francois' full mouth or the thick, hard shape lying across his thigh and reproducing it on her sketch paper. There's no moistening of her pussy, no pulsating urges nagging and fretting when she hears Suki's moans growing to abandoned screeches of pleasure as he fucks her.

No one knows this. Not even Suki: but Kara has not had a man since she lost her virginity.

She's forgotten to breathe. She bursts out of the water like a seal, gasping and groping for the edge of the pool.

But instead of getting a grip on the hot paving stones her fingers are grabbed and she is pulled right up out of the water by someone very strong.

"You have five minutes to get out. This is private property!"

Through the vision blurred by chlorine she sees a large, dark man glaring at her, his arms crossed aggressively over his immaculately pressed pale pink shirt. Kara starts shivering, even though the sun is drying the water off her skin. The contrast in temperature makes her nipples harden.

"Francois said you were away," she stammers, bowing to pick up her towel. "We're staying next door, and it's a shit hole, there's no electricity, and spiders, and so—"

"You can lay off the poor sweet thing, Henri. I've located Francois and he tells me these girls are his friends!"

A tall woman with black hair piled in an elegant coil, huge sunglasses and a see-through white kaftan wafts down the lawn.

The man's black eyes graze over Kara's naked body as he pushes his Panama hat back over his thick greying hair.

"Francois? What's he doing here?" The man gestures angrily at the woman and at the house. "He's supposed to be working, not freeloading with a brace of topless tarts just when we've driven all the way through France to get the place ready for our party."

"I'm so sorry. I'll go get Suki and we'll make ourselves scarce." Kara bunches the towel around her bare breasts but then drops her sketchpad and pencils. "I ... I promise we haven't damaged or stolen anything."

The man opens his mouth to retort, but the woman gestures imperiously, ordering him back up to the villa. Then she steps forward to retrieve Kara's sketchpad.

"You'll blow a gasket with all this shouting, Henri. Just go and sort out our son. And while you're at it, I give you permission to punish the cute little bint he's been busy screwing in our bed. I'll deal with this rather lovely intruder." She glances at Kara, and then the semi-nude drawing of the guy who turns out *not* to be the pool boy. "The anatomical detail here is exquisite. You have a real skill here."

A deep flush rises in Kara's face and spreads through her body. The slow, husky way the woman speaks gives everything a delicious *double entendre*.

"The bint and I are graduates from art school. We're spending the summer preparing a portfolio to present to London galleries. We're staying next door

"Really." The woman keeps her eyes on Kara. Her husband flings his arms in the air and turns to storm up to the house, muttering *"putain"* and "cul" under his breath. As soon as the man has disappeared into the shadows the woman's vivid red lipsticked smile lights up her café crème coloured skin.

"Now that my brute of a husband has gotten that off his chest, let's start again, shall we? Finding two gorgeous intruders in the house is far more interesting than talking about what canapés we'll be serving tomorrow night. And I meant what I said about your artwork. I can introduce you to a friend of mine who has a gallery up in St. Paul de Vence."

Kara shakes her head and holds out her hand for the sketches. "That's very kind, but we've taken enough of your hospitality already."

The woman reaches out and strokes Kara's face.

"Don't look so worried, *cherie*. Henri's bark is worse than his bite. We've driven all the way.

from Paris today. He's exhausted and grumpy, that's all. *Et moi?* I am just dying to cool off!"

The woman suddenly slips off her kaftan. Beneath it she is wearing a kind of Fifties starlet style bathing suit in sugar white. Her large breasts pillow out of the corseted top, a frilled skirt flares over her tanned thighs. She looks like a glorious lily.

"So … I'll get out of your hair," Kara murmurs, reaching out again to take her drawing materials. "You'll not see us again."

"And wouldn't that be a crying shame."

The lady places the pad and pencil down on the table, takes Kara's hand, and before either of them can say another word she jumps with her into the pool. The water washes over her hot body as the lady pulls her along and then duck-dives under the surface.

Kara re-emerges and hovers by the edge, watching the wavering lines of the woman's body beneath the water. The lady suddenly springs up, scattering diamond drops, black hair sleek against her scalp, emphasising her enormous Cleopatra eyes outlined in what must be waterproof eyeliner.

"This outfit is really for posing," she splutters, waving her hands in the air like a synchronised swimmer. "The chlorine will ruin it. I'm going to take it off. Can you unzip me, um …?"

"Kara."

"And I'm Odette. My husband is Henri, and our naughty son is Francois."

The two women remain in the water, submerged to their shoulders. Odette wades to Kara, turning as she lifts the tendrils of black hair escaping down her long neck. Kara hesitates, then slowly unzips the white bodice so it falls open. Odette doesn't move. So Kara unpeels the suit, with some difficulty, away from her body. It is very tight, and it sticks to her wet skin. Kara brings her hands round to the front to yank it down and the luscious double swell of breasts bounces against her fingers. Her heart jumps in her throat. Odette moves slightly, and the costume slips right off.

"It's alright" Odette chuckles. "You can touch them if you like."

Odette catches Kara's fingers and brushes them over her breasts. Even under the water Kara can feel how big and firm they are, and when she squeezes them her own breasts tingle fiercely in response. She's squeezing hard. She expects Odette to fling herself away, but instead her head tips back slightly, resting on Kara's shoulder.

Kara's mouth is open as she struggles not to pant out loud as new, frantic lust floods through her like rain falling on the dry desert of her life. Odette turns her head and her cheek presses against Kara's mouth. She kisses it. Those big soft breasts pushing into her hands are twisting Kara's stomach into knots and her cunt twitches violently.

Odette turns her head a little more and, when her lips meet Kara's to taste the immediate responding warmth, she turns around fully. Her mouth is gentle, just resting there, but as their breasts are squashed against each other Kara can feel longing tightening in her throat as Odette sways from side to side, her hard cold nipples rubbing fire into Kara's.

"My god, what are you doing to me, young Kara? I haven't touched another woman like this for years."

Odette's lower half is shimmering almost green like a mermaid under the water as she pulls Kara over to the side. Kara floats helplessly after this sexy siren. She can't take her eyes off the molasses black hair, eyes like a witch, the fluid body, and that red smiling mouth that she just wants to kiss again and again.

"You are so beautiful, Odette," Kara murmurs, and she does kiss her. Really kisses her, as if she's a boy, and Odette is her girl, but softer than a boy would kiss, sweeter. It has the same electrifying effect, though. Her lips rest on Odette's, sliding gently until they start to tingle. She can feel the wetness of Odette's tongue now. She feels wanton and rough as she pushes Odette against the tiled side of the pool. The older woman pulls free and stretches her arms along the edge. Her limbs are lithe and feathery as the water laps around them, but her breasts bobbing on the surface are firm like fruit.

A sudden noisy clattering of pots and pans from the kitchen is followed not by raised voices but a sudden burst of dance music. Odette's lips are still parted, her tongue tucked into the corner of her mouth if she's finishing a sugary doughnut. She winks at Kara and arches her back. She's offering herself. Kara's nipples start to ache with wanting as their hands meet across the water.

Odette is staring at Kara's panting mouth. The wicked expression in her eyes and the moist parting of her lips sends lightning through Kara's belly. Her head is spinning with the sun on her head, the chill of the water, the flashing of this woman's eyes. She smiles with her whole body, her eyelashes fluttering. She is flirting with her hostess. Odette winds one leg round the back of Kara's thighs to stop her floating away.

They are up close again, as if this is where they have always been. Eyes closed, breasts pressed together. Kara tickles Odette's lips with the tip of her tongue; and with a low, soft moan of pleasure Odette wraps her arms round Kara and pushes her soft wet tongue into Kara's mouth so they are sucking on each other, neither of them worried about who might see. It must look pretty damn hot because it sure feels perfect. They jerk and writhe in a kind of dance. Odette keeps her leg hooked round Kara, pushing closer. Her pussy rubs on Kara's, and it's delicious.

Kara has touched herself so many times in the dark but she's had no one to envisage. No one to fuel her fantasies. There's nothing to compare to someone else's body, someone else's fingers on you. She is pulsing down there. Her heat, her honey must be mingling with the pool water. God, she wants this woman.

"We've come to an agreement!"

Henri's voice booms from the terrace. Odette and Kara part reluctantly, and spin lazily round to rest their chins on their arms as Henri and a hectically flushed Suki come dancing down the lawn. "Where's Francois?" Kara whispers, using the excuse to nibble Odette's ear.

Odette flutters her eyelashes against Kara's cheek, making Kara shudder with renewed pleasure. "Henri's probably elbowed him out of the way and tasted your friend for himself. So there's no need to feel any guilt for what I'm going to do to you later."

Henri kicks off his shorts and shirt and dives right over their heads into the pool. Suki watches him with undisguised admiration then plunges in after him.

The master of the house surfaces at last, with Suki hanging on to his huge shoulders like a baby monkey.

"These two cute little kittens can stay with us on one condition." Henri lifts Suki bodily out of the water and the playfully drops her back in. "That they serve the drinks at the party tomorrow night."

Kara tries to catch her friend's eye, but the world has shifted and gone mad. Everyone has changed places.

Their two faces are wide eyed in the huge hall mirror. Fairy lights are twinkling all around the twilit garden. Tables are laid with food and wine, and huge cushions are scattered all over the lawns and under the trees for the guests. A crunching of gravel on the drive announces the first chauffeurs delivering their VIPs from Cap Ferrat and St. Tropez.

"Is this a dream, K?" asks Suki, running her finger around the rosebud lips that Kara has just painted pink to match Suki's pale pink mini dress. "This house is like some kind of enchanted castle. Henri's a kind of Bluebeard. Odette is the wicked stepmother. Francois is the handsome prince—"

"And we are the damsels in de dresses!" Kara tweaks her strappy sea green sheath just enough to show the eager swell of her tits. Tonight has to be the night that Odette sucks on those. She picks up her tray of glasses. "It's real life on the Riviera, Suki, and I for one can't get enough!"

They take their positions on either side of the

garden door, hopping excitedly on their high heels. The swimming pool is floodlit and rows of iron braziers, their flames standing straight up and barely flickering in the balmy air, make a fiery path across the lawn towards a little gate which leads down to the private beach where Francois is firing up the barbecue for his friends.

The evening spins past in an tipsy whirl of famous faces. Suki hands out drinks and canapés for about an hour, then disappears down to the beach. Kara takes her role more seriously, especially as she is being watched by both Monsieur and Madame, but she prefers to stay near the pool. Her feet in the killer heels are killing her and she wonders when she can kick them off.

"You look ravishing *ce soir, cherie.*" Kara feels something soft pressing up against her arm. She looks down to see large, round breasts encased in scarlet lace. The sophisticated lady of the manor looks exotic and dangerous tonight in a tight, red dress. "I've been counting the minutes until I can get you to myself."

This simple, sexy remark, in Odette's throaty voice makes Kara spark with startling, intense pleasure. She can't take her eyes off the breasts spilling out of the lace. Lust stirs inside her as she compares Odette's luscious, nut-brown pair—and that dark, inviting valley between them—with her own paler cleavage.

"I'm flattered," she murmurs. "You're pretty sensational yourself."

"Come on then. I dare you to do something outrageous." Odette glances at her remaining guests, her plump lips parted in a huge grin. Kara has an unsettling image of them wrapped round a giant phallus, giving stupendous head. No doubt that's what every man thinks when he looks at Odette's mouth. "I'll race you to the pool."

Kara hesitates. Most of the guests are either down on the beach or have left. At this precise moment there is no-one around. She lifts her dress over her knees and races after Odette's brown, toned legs. They push past a knot of drunken couples and reach the edge of the glittering oval pool. It's so enticing in the moonlight, sparkling turquoise liquid illuminated by the underwater floodlights. Some rhythmic music throbs from inside the open plan sitting room whose doors are open to the terrace

"Henri has a terrible taste in music," giggles Odette, grabbing Kara, and before Kara can take a breath she is pulled fully clothed into the water with a shriek and a splash. The water is body heat. Steam rises towards the already black sky. The water laps at her gently as Odette swims underneath and springs up in front of her, black hair sleek against her scalp, emphasising her enormous eyes and making her look even more mysterious, not less.

More familiar, not less. Kara has been unable to think of anyone but Odette for the last two days.

"Best to take this lovely dress off, *cherie*. It will

survive if it's not in the chlorine for too long."

The mistress of the house turns and lifts her long wet hair. She doesn't have to say any more. Kara eagerly unzips her red lace dress. Odette doesn't move, so Kara pushes the dress off her shoulders. It clings as tightly as the bathing suit did, and is even more delicate. It must be already ruined. Kara fiddles at the buttons at the front of the dress and it suddenly slips off, so that her fingers brush against Odette's breasts once again. The lust twangs so sharply inside, communicates so directly to her own nipples, that she bites down on her lip. Odette's head tips slightly, obviously aroused by the contact. God, Kara wants to touch her. She wants to go much further than that this time.

"So touch me" says Odette, as if Kara has spoken out loud. "Let them watch. It's why they come to these parties. Touch my breasts, *cherie.*" She presses herself, curvy and soft, into Kara's hands for a moment. Really lingers, her lips parted with lazy pleasure as if she and Kara already know each other intimately.

Then she dodges sideways, pulls her red dress right off and tosses it onto a lounger.

"Show them how sexy you are. They're all watching. This is a pool party, *cherie.* Let yourself go!"

She pulls off Kara's dainty dress, then kisses her on the lips. As she swims away from her through the steaming water Kara gazes at her bare shoulders, the stretch of her neck, the black hair streaming back. Again there's the sensation that she's known this woman all her life. She glances up. They are not alone. Some of the guests have noticed movement in the pool, the two naked women circling one another.

Odette reaches the deep end and rests against the tiled side, arms outstretched along the edge, her big tits bobbing like air-filled buoys on the surface of the water. Steam rises as the water shifts, her breasts teasing in and out of the water.

Excitement kicks inside Kara's belly. The other guests are pretending not to watch as they help themselves to the drinks still left on the trays. Francois, Suki, and some other youngsters are still on the beach. The rest of the staff have gone home.

Odette is on a mission. She beckons Kara over and wraps her arms round Kara's waist. Kara knows she's not the first woman Odette has played with like this. She wonders what the others are, or were, like. Is it her red hair that attracts Odette? Her white, limber body? Or just something behind the eyes that has woken up and said *come and get me?*

Odette has probably tried everything under the sun at least once. And that's what Kara wants to do.

The two women's faces are up close. Kara runs her hands over Odette's hips, over her ribcage. She can feel no bone, just soft, yielding flesh, and then those gorgeous breasts nuzzling into her hands. That's why they are called puppies! She looks down, pinches the long brown nipples into stiffness, and her own grow hard as nuts as if they are being fondled as well. As Kara teases each taut tip, Odette arches her back so that everyone can see what Kara is doing to her.

Odette's legs encircle Kara's waist and their two bodies, two pussies, brush together. Kara smiles. Puppies and pussies. How cute is that? Hard nipple scrapes across hard nipple and the tight ball of desire inside Kara starts to unravel.

Odette wraps her arms around Kara's neck and kisses her, her big, generous lips tickling, her tongue flicking. Kara sucks the older woman's tongue into her mouth and as they circle in the steaming water they writhe and grind against each other, pussy lips parting, burning clits emerging, seeking friction.

Kara keeps her eyes closed, imagining the watching faces, but what she doesn't expect is audience participation. Suddenly there's a mighty splash at the other end of the pool. The women pause then pull apart slowly, allowing their tongues to linger in a little slick of saliva, before they turn lazily to see who is joining them. Another girl, perhaps?

Henri is swimming across the pool, already naked. The handful of guests are gathered round the pool, sitting on loungers or standing, intrigued by the promise of aqueous synchrony.

"Where's little Suki?" Henri asks, coming up behind his wife. Kara experiences a furious jolt of frustration as her interrupted excitement starts to ebb away. "Is she on the beach?"

"Who cares? You're interrupting us, Henri. Go away," Odette snaps, winking at Kara.

Henri takes hold of Odette's shoulders and gives them a little shake. "Did you know Serge has decided to show up, too? He'll never miss a free party. He was going straight down to the beach find Francois."

Odette stretches her arm towards Kara. "How lovely! The whole family together!"

"But Suki won't know they're brothers, will she? What if there's a fight?"

"You better get your big stick out, Henri, get down there and stop them if you want her for yourself?"

But Henri doesn't move. His hands slide off Odette's shoulders, down her sides and under the water. "My big stick is already out, Odette. You better watch out."

Kara's frustration coils into jealousy as he pushes himself against his wife and there's an answering leap of desire in Odette's eyes.

"I thought you weren't into anything over thirty these days?" taunts Odette as her husband's big hands reappear to stroke her breasts. "After all, I'm *only* your wife."

"Yes, but something has fired up your lagging appetite since we arrived here."

The competition, now that Henri has joined them, makes Kara all the more determined to win back Odette's attention. Under the cover of the water she edges her hand between Odette's legs, parting the soft lips with her fingers. Smiling and gasping with surprise Odette falls back against Henri, hooking her ankles loosely round Kara's thighs so that her body rises to the surface of the pool like an offering.

"I'm tempted to stay right here," Henri replies, hands moving possessively over his wife's breasts. The guests crane forwards, and another man Kara hasn't seen before, casually dressed, pulls off his shorts and Breton jersey and dives in to the pool. Kara assumes everyone will join now, but the others stay on dry land, assuming this is all part of the entertainment.

The new guy swims up and circles them like a shark. Henri looks so astonished that he doesn't stop his thickset, unshaven rival, from joining in. Kara can see there's some kind of power struggle going on between the two men, but she has her own power struggle going on now. She wants to fight them for Odette's lovely body. Pushing her fingers inside Odette, she leans forward over Odette's bare belly, pushes Henri's hand out of the way and bites down on one taut nipple. Henri and the other man fall away to watch. The bud enters Kara's mouth, thrusting up against her teeth, and Kara sucks on it, blinded by the wicked excitement searing through her.

There's an answering pull on her fingers as Odette's cunt tightens. She starts to fidget in the water, and Kara sucks harder on the tight nipples, thrusting her fingers in and out of Odette until she comes, moaning in surprise, her head splashing back in the water.

Everyone on the edge of the pool starts clapping.

The two men waste no time in tugging Kara and a limp Odette to the shallow end. Maybe now's the time to scramble out of the pool. But the men are just getting started. The shallower the water gets, the higher their torsos rise from the water, until Henri's cock shoots upwards out of the water and bangs against Odette's face. At the same time, the second man comes up behind Kara, his big hands on her hips. She tries to pull away, but Henri shakes his head.

"You stay right there and do as you're told," he says, cradling Odette so that she is floating on her back in front of him. "And watch what I do to my wife when she has been naughty."

Standing to one side of Odette, Henri pokes the swollen head of his massive dick into the corner of her mouth.

For a moment Odette remains motionless as if she is asleep, then her mouth opens slowly. Her tongue slips out and welcomes the round knob, sucking it in. Those lips that Kara was just kissing, and so beautifully made for blowjobs, start pulling on her husband's stiff cock. Not even an expert mouth like hers could take in the entire length without choking, and the sight of at least a third of his length sliding in and out of Odette's mouth turns Kara to jelly as she absently strokes Odette's legs.

She wants to be out of the pool, on a big warm bed away from everybody, rolling her body to fit with Odette's. She wants to abandon herself to the experience of feeling Odette's big lips kissing her again, going down on her snatch, nibbling her clit, tonguing her cunt—she wants it all.

But she's not going to get it, at least not this minute, because the other man has pushed up and bent her over Odette's prone body so that now her face is between Odette's floating thighs. She kisses the other woman there, parting her legs to reveal the plump, delicious crevice; and as she bends to lick her mistress, the second man pulls Kara's legs apart and she's so excited and so wet that when he pushes himself inside she is ready.

Kara tries to focus on licking her lovely Odette but she is losing control. Her aroused body responds to the man's brutal, rough stimulation. His big fingers under the water somehow muffle the roughness, but a fierce renewed lust still kicks inside her.

Her bottom is tipped up out of the water and into

the air for everyone to see. The man opens her up, pushes his hard cock into her. Then, as her body loosens and lets him in, his strong hands rock her violently back and forth as he thrusts hard and fast, and now all Kara can think about and see and hear are her own groans of lust, Odette's muffled moans, and the bestial grunting of the men.

"*Doucement*," growls the man in Kara's ear. "God, you feel as good as our hostess!"

Kara's not sure she's heard right, but she can't think further than the cock filling her, its accelerating, determined thrusts, pushing her forwards so that her face grinds into Odette's pussy. What an incredible combination they must make. Two men, two women. A sexual chain, a novel kind of line dance. The working parts of a sex machine.

Kara gives herself up to this debauchery. Odette is in her hands. Everything is fine. More than fine. Odette opens her mouth to show us the stream of her husband's cum and that starts the chain reaction of the others, until they are all coming, lifting and splashing in the water in a shuddering sequence.

There is a brief silence, just the panting of the participants and the splashing of the water against the edge of the pool. Then the laughter and clapping starts again. The men swim silently to the edge, shaking the water from their hair. Kara edges herself up close to Odette even as the men climb out of the pool, their buttocks taut and muscled, their heavy cocks and juicy balls still bouncing and swinging as they strut to the chairs to pick up their clothes.

"Who the hell was that?" Kara gasps, pointing at the rough guy now giving a jovial high five to Henri.

"That's my friend with the art gallery," laughs Odette, kissing her softly and reaching for a towel. "Come and meet him properly!"

◆ ◆ ◆ ◆

Down on the beach the barbecue has been abandoned, the remains of steaks and salads and beer bottles cluster here and there amid shreds of aromatic smoke. The sea is a dark silky sheet with frills of foamy white as the waves turn on the beach. Suki is on her own, knee deep in the shallows, lifting her pale pink dress right over her bare butt and shivering as cold droplets touch her skin. Francois and this older boy who turned up earlier in a white motorboat are frolicking further out, ducking and diving and obviously vying for her attention.

Suki is sulking slightly, because Henri went up to the house ages ago and hasn't come back. She likes knowing he is watching her all the time. She has never been fucked by someone old enough to be her father before, and last night, when he came and stole her from the bedroom she shared with Kara while the others were sleeping, was mind-blowing.

She is just kicking at the waves when she feels herself hoisted into the air like a doll and carried over to a rug on the beach beside the embers of a bonfire. She is handed a cold beer and, with a few chunks of wood, the fire quickly blazes to life once more.

Suki sighs, relaxing as the beer hits her blood stream. The rest of the gang are playing cards up the other end of the beach.

"So who is this?" she asks, pointing at the newcomer. "How do you two know each other?"

They exchange glances. "This is Serge. We, er, we grew up together."

Suki smiles. They are both pretty gorgeous. All the more so in this flickering light. She can't stay still. The taller boy, Serge, is pulling off his wet shirt and soaking jeans, revealing a pair of equally wet, clinging boxers. The boxers stay on. Suki crawls across to Francois and tweaks at the buttons of his shirt.

"We may as well all get naked," she giggles. "What do you think?"

The boys exchange glances. The older one flushes and bites back a grin, before busying himself with tidying up the mess. Maybe they haven't understood her. Suki glances up at the sky, which looks black and thick with cloud. A slight breeze is cutting of the sea and she shivers.

"Well, I'm taking this wet dress off before I catch a chill."

She pulls the dress easily over her head and lays it out flat on the sand. Francois' brown eyes are like saucers and she shivers again, this time with pleasure, as she releases her breasts from her bra.

"Come and lie down," she says, crawling over to Francois and pushing him down onto his back. The bonfire is warm on her skin now, and when they lie down they are sheltered from the breeze. Francois lets her push him down on to his back. She can't resist him any longer. She crawls over his prone body, rubbing herself up his legs, pausing over the cock that is rearing so eagerly, effortlessly tenting the soft fabric of his shorts. She pretends to ignore it, continues to slither up his stomach, until she's on all fours poised over his face.

Francois grabs her buttocks. They haven't done this before. Very slowly Suki lowers herself until her pussy is against his mouth, and as she rocks herself gently her soft wet pussy brushes against his lips. A moan escapes her, even though she's trying to be cool and in control. Francois tries to lick her, and she is desperate to sink down on to his face, but she wants to tease him. Actually she's teasing herself more by holding herself away.

She glances up at the cliffs and the sandy path for signs of Henri. But he's not coming back. A mixture of annoyance and determination surges through her. So she'll take her pleasure right here, and if he comes down and catches her with his precious son, well, so much the better!

She sinks down at last, tossing her head back with delight as Francois digs his fingers into her flesh. She wriggles into his face and he obediently starts to lick at her. The fluttering of nerves and anger in her stomach tightens into a clump of fierce desire. She spreads her legs a little wider, opens herself to the searching tongue, relishing the tiny sensations pricked and building all through her.

With a huge wrench of will she pulls herself away from his face and moves down so that now her breasts hang in his face. She knows he likes this. She watches his fingers moulding her breasts, wandering across them and squeezing, pushing them together, letting them fall, playing with them, his young face staring at the rigid raspberry nipples. She pushes them invitingly at his mouth. His breath whistles against her flesh.

Forget any teenage gropings Francois might have had before. I wonder if he's done this in front of his friends? Not with a brazen English girl, surely? She wants him and his father to remember her. She wants this summer to be the best they ever had.

And in a way this is a first for her. Playing the older woman. She wants to smother Francois, keep him there. With swift, deft fingers, Suki soon has him naked too. And he nuzzles his gratitude between her breasts. Suki wants to slow it down, let him to relish every moment of this so he will always compare her to the other girls and she will be queen. She rubs one taut dark nipple across his mouth.

The tip of his tongue flicks out tentatively. Suki's knees wobble, and she clutches more firmly to his shoulders, to keep her balance and to keep him in place, her nipple angled right into his mouth.

His tongue flicks again and his hands squeeze her breasts until they sing with delicious pain. At last, at last, he nibbles it, the tongue lapping round, drawing the burning bud into his mouth, pulling hard on it as he begins to suck. Suki gazes at his long tangled hair, the salt water dried in granules and flecked white across his cheek bones. She's not sure if she loves him, but she loves all this. She wants to stay forever. She looks away over his head, across the dark hump of the dunes and over the ocean, up at the deserted cliffs. The older boy seems to have vanished.

She experiments with the idea of distancing herself from what is happening, but Francois knows her well now, his mouth, his teeth, keep pulling the aching nipple, pulling her attention back.

Charges of electricity streak through her body to her empty, waiting cunt.

He has the other breast up by his face and turns his head this way and that, lapping and sucking, snuffling through his nose to breathe, groaning, biting and kneading harder and harder as if he owns her breasts. This is real, selfish satisfaction for both of them.

Suki pushes herself more roughly against him, seeking, searching for more pain at her nipples to communicate more pleasure through the rest of her. She parts her legs and lifts her knees to plant them on either side of his thighs so that she is straddling him, and still she has his head crushed between her tits. She tilts her wet pussy desperately towards his groin and rubs it briefly against his cock. It pulses against her, thumping free from the rough tangle of curls, pulsating golden brown like the rest of him, its surface smooth like velvet, the mauve plum emerging to show itself to her as the soft foreskin retreats.

Suki folds her fingers round it and its owner bites her nipple so hard that she screams delight, leaning over him and settling herself just above her new toy.

"Just take a little break," she whispers. She starts to wriggle back down his body so that his head follows for a moment, still nibbling at her nipples, but then he falls back as she slithers down towards his groin. He can only grab at her wet hair. Her face reaches his young cock, standing up like a beacon. The tip is already beading in anticipation and she opens her mouth and draws it in with her teeth and tongue until the knob knocks at the back of her throat.

He gasps, exquisitely shocked. His buttocks clench as she sucks on him, nibbling down, licking and sucking the sweet length of it. He starts bucking gently, crying out in amazement. Suki wonders if his pert little girlfriends give head like this, and doubts it. After all, *she* didn't have a clue at that age! She hopes he'll think he's died and gone to heaven. Any minute now she is going to heaven, too.

She's just preparing the way. As she sucks she rubs her tits against him, grinds her pussy into his leg. He pulls at her hair, and she has to slow herself down. She doesn't want to waste this golden moment by coming all over his thighs. Her pussy is contracting frantically now, and she's leaving a slick of juice wherever her naked pussy has been.

She gives one last, long suck, pulling it towards her throat and nipping it with her teeth, then she lets it slide out past her teeth, along her tongue and out into her waiting hand. She starts to rise, and he pushes up on his elbows, seeking her tits again, but she presses him gently down on his back. She leans toward him, with his cock standing proud and slick and needy between them

"See how beautiful it is," she coos, showing him the length of his cock encircled by her fingers and glistening with her lick.

She smiles as he watches her rise on her knees. She aims his cock towards her soft centre and lets it rest just there, at the entrance, nudging past the wet sex lips. At last she lowers herself a little more, gasping as each inch goes in, then she reaches under him and cups his balls, making him groan again. The tension is ecstasy, but she can't hold on for much longer, and slowly, luxuriously, Suki lets the boy's smooth, fat bulb slide all the way up inside her. It is tempting to ride it, to ram down on it over and over, but she forces herself to pull out again. He frowns but she eases herself down again, moaning and tossing her head back, and the next time she does it he is with her, pulling his own hips back, waiting when she waits.

His eyes are on hers again, but as she sighs with the delight of being filled, and bends over to let her tits swing across his mouth again, his eyes flip sideways. His hands come up to her hips and hold her still. She doesn't move. She doesn't want to, and she can't, but then he pulls her nipples back into her mouth, raising her butt in the air as they start their rhythm again. If they do this much longer she's going to come. Her inner muscles are tightening each time to grab hold and keep him inside her, and his cock gets harder with each thrust. She's just poised to ram herself down onto him harder than ever when she feels the cheeks of her ass cupped and pulled apart as the warmth of another male body presses up against her back.

"*Excusez moi*," someone says. "May I?"

Suki is too astonished to answer. Francois frowns and shakes his head, but the other boy takes hold of her anyway.

"*Je suis son frère. Serge.*"

Suki's jumbled brain takes in the words and she squeals with shocked laughter as she realises that these two are brothers. So either there's no such thing as sibling rivalry and these brothers have the same easy relationship that she has with Kara. Or there's going to be some fierce competition with her as the prize.

Too many different sensations are swirling through

her to allow much thought and she allows herself to be manhandled. She's pulled, first forwards, her tits licked and sucked to burning point by her accomplished pupil, and then tugged backwards by his invisible brother, who now has his own stiff cock wedged up between her cheeks and he is sliding it up and down the warm crack. He guides it lower, sliding right under her, soaking in her honey, jousting and jostling alongside where his brother has already spliced her open. Such a confusion of cock feels lewd and immoral, and both cocks are slick with her dew. One big dick inside her, the shaft of the other grazing her swollen pussy lips while its head nudges her exposed clitoris. Suki's is dizzy now. She doesn't know which part of her is which. Everything is fizzing and burning as she dances on her boy's cock, flinging herself wildly about as the urge for satisfaction and the loss of her previous control start to overtake her.

Both brothers take hold of her then and make her stop, and the pause is as titillating as the wild movement, because all her muscles keep on working. Francois takes her arms and pulls them taut above his head so that she is suspended above him. Her breasts in his face, he goes on suckling her nipples, but he stops his thrusting for a moment and she lets the hovering orgasm recede a little while they wait.

Then Serge the invisible brother brings his stiff cock once again to the cleft of her ass. She can feel how slippery he is—how slippery she has made him. This time, instead of letting his penis slide down along the crack, he starts to push it toward the puckered hole of her anus. She goes rigid. She can feel the hole tightening like a fist against the intrusion, but at the same time a throb ignites like a pilot light somewhere inside her vagina, just the other side, she supposes, of that thin wall separating the two openings. Christ, what's happening now? Is this even physically possible? Who's the teacher now?

She's never had a threesome, despite what she's boasted to Kara. And certainly not been the plaything of a father and his two sons.

The throbbing deep inside is threatening to explode as the other secret part of her opens to its invader. Serge's thick tip pushes in a fraction. Her own shy muscles try to push it out at first, and then slacken to accommodate him, welcoming the male hardness, so that inch by inch it grinds up her backside.

She can't think, she can't breathe. She has two thick cocks wedged inside her, impaling her, and she's embracing them both, straining to keep them there and to milk them for all the hot pleasure they have to offer.

They are all three very still for a moment, introducing their bodies to each other. And as they pause, there's a rumble of thunder far away in the mountains and a noticeable shivering in the air.

Serge is deep inside now. His thighs are propping up her own, and he starts to rock, his breath hot on her neck, one big hand fanned out against her stomach to support them both in that position, and she lets the rocking move her body, carefully at first, still unsure of how the complicated design of her body can manage this, whether it will hurt or damage, but then she relaxes as her body becomes conflicting zones of exquisite pleasure.

A fat cold drop of rain falls on her neck. Another on her shoulder. A rapid spattering on her back. The sand pops with rain as if a sniper is firing at them from the cliffs.

The boys swear under their breath and move faster.

Suki falls first forwards onto the rigid cock inside her cunt, then back onto the one in her butt, and it's fiery now, jets of fire burning her everywhere. As she moves off one brother the other brother penetrates her. The storm of orgasm gathers along with the thunder shouting over their heads now. The grunting of both the boys and her own moans rise into the heavy sea air from somewhere in her throat and are snatched away to mingle with the steady shower.

And then it's happening, she's shrieking and shivering with the cold rain on her skin and the heat building inside her. All three of them are rocking frantically, both boys ramming their cocks into her in unison so that she spirals on to them at the same time, welcoming the burning heat, Francois falling back on the rug when he can hold his seed back no longer. The explosion comes spurting out of him, met by her own gripping, convulsive orgasm.

Serge laughs and yells as their friends come running up from the other end of the beach, just in time to catch him bringing up the rear in this debauched mêlée.

Suki's legs are shaking with the effort of keeping upright and she topples sideways. The boys jump up, throw her clothes at her, then rush around packing up everything that needs to get out of the rain. She lies back on the rug, letting the rain soak into her, and that's when she notices the row of watching figures standing on the cliff top above. Henri and another man have their arms crossed. Odette and Kara have their arms around each other. The other guests either beam with delight, or have mouths agape in awe at the exhibition they have just witnessed.

Francois and Serge wave at their audience. Their friends run up the cliff ahead of them but are virtually ignored by Henri and Odette, who keep their eyes fixed on Suki and the brothers.

She is going to be greeted by her hosts either with fury or fanfare, Suki can't tell which. She'll find out soon enough. The brothers grab each of her hands and together they all run, laughing, across the sand, up the stony path, and into the fairy-lit villa.

N A I A D

◆◆◆◆

By

JUSTINE ELYOT

N a i a d

◆◆◆◆

The others were sleeping off their hangovers, still fully dressed on the collapsing cane furniture. None of them stirred when I opened the wooden shutters to admit sunlight to the bottle strewn floor, though Louis grunted a bit, so I went down to the boathouse on my own.

The boathouse was underneath the villa, a kind of basement garage built from crazy paving with two arched exits for the boats. I didn't really want to speed around the lake today so I killed the motor once I'd made it a few hundred yards from the villa and lay down in my wooden shell, having no ambition beyond an hour's drifting under the mid-morning Mittel-European sun.

From here, I could see the villa in all its tumbledown glory, crouching beneath its canopy of trees as if preparing to lurch into the lake. It was falling apart, but that was why it was cheap, and it had that certain faded grandeur so often seen in old buildings around here. What was it with the Austro-Hungarians and the colour yellow though? Did every building have to be that same shade of ochre?

I pushed my bare toes down against the sandy wood. It was warm and I felt like a basking flounder, lying there in my crochet cover-up and bikini bottoms. I put my sunhat over my face and let the boat go where it liked, drifting along and rocking in rhythm with it, my body merging into the sunlicked warmth.

The next time I took my hat off my face, the boat had moseyed its way past the trees that stood out in the lake, demarcating the space between our property and the next. Now I had an unimpeded view of the vacant villa next door, and much more salubrious than our shack it was too. Again, that yellow of the old empire, but the windows were new and the paintwork was smart and everything looked well tended and ornamental. It had a boathouse of its own, a dark wood pagoda with all kinds of gothic touches. Balconies and arched windows and a little turret and all.

Frau Metternich had told us the owner was rarely there except in August, when he spent the month. It seemed ridiculous that one man should require all that space, but apparently he had no family, although he gave extravagant parties there. I imagined the late lazy summer evenings, fireflies skimming the water, jazz music wafting over the lake, loosened tuxedo collars, women running across the lawn with stiletto straps hanging from their fingers.

In June the place was deserted. Nobody there. Blank windows gazed down upon me and I felt like saluting them back.

I sat up. I was hot. The sun was climbing to its zenith and my skin was starting to tighten under its unforgiving glare.

Nobody was around to see me. I shimmied out of my cover-up, hesitated for a moment, then took off my bikini bottoms. In seconds, I was over the side, a mermaid sluicing through the warm, slightly weedy water. I felt fronds tickle and touch my thighs and I swirled past them, imagining myself on a mission, ducking and curling and flailing through the aqua waters. When my limbs tired, I arranged myself into a starfish float and lay there, lapped and led and tilted by the wavelets, looking at the bleached light on the insides of my eyelids and telling myself that Louis wasn't worth it … he wasn't worth it … none of it was worth it …

"Where is your gold?"

The voice was male and spoke in German.

My limbs retracted into cramped flappers and I got a mouthful of sluggish water that almost choked me. I coughed hard, tread water and looked at the source of the question.

I had drifted closer to that crazy gothic boathouse, where a man smiled down at me from the landing stage beside it. He was older but attractive, expensively dressed in pale linen. Shit. The owner of the villa—it had to be. Was I trespassing, swimming here? Could I get into trouble?

Then I thought of what he had said. What the hell was it supposed to mean?

"I'm sorry," I said, also in German. "Gold?"

"Then you are not a Rhinemaiden?" he said.

Ah. I understood now. A reference to the watery guardians of the Rhinegold, famous in Wagner's Ring Cycle.

"I don't think so," I said. "Just a common or garden naiad."

He laughed at that.

"I'm delighted to find one in my lake," he said. "I've always wanted one."

His face was youthful in its expressiveness, though it was impossible to place his age. His eyes were dark and watched me as if they could direct my movements, bringing me up out of the water to him.

They were covetous, I thought. It ought to have scared me, but it didn't at all.

"I hope I'm not trespassing," I said, ready to plunge into a frantic backstroke if his answer wasn't friendly.

"Not at all. You are a naiad. The water belongs to you. But there might be a small penalty for coming so close to my property."

His face drew me towards it. Whatever the penalty was, I wanted to pay it.

"What is it?"

"You have to come up here and have a drink with me."

I twisted my neck back to the boat. It was a good five hundred yards away, and so were my clothes.

"Now?" I asked.

"Now," he said, with the kind of authority that suggested there was no alternative.

And perhaps it was the sun, or my scrambled state of mind after last night's drama, or just a moment of sheer and florid madness, but I didn't care that I was naked. I began to swim towards him until I found footing, and then I walked slowly, gathering weeds as I went, towards the lake side.

I wished I could see myself as he must see me, emerging from the lake with green fronds hanging like wet ribbons over my breasts and hips, my hair dripping beads on to my skin.

It certainly seemed to have its effect on him, anyway. I watched him as he watched me and his eyes flickered from ironically amused to astonished to avid in a series of intricate widenings and narrowings.

"My god," he said, reaching out a hand to help me up into the soft reedy mud. "You really *are* a water nymph, aren't you?"

"Yes," I said, deciding in that moment that I would be. Just for the duration of this encounter, I would liberate myself from everything that pinned me into my established identity. Not Jessie Wright, fretting about her unfaithful boyfriend and her PhD on the cultural legacy of Ludwig the Mad of Bavaria. Just this body, rising from the lake, to meet this strangely compelling man.

"Well," he said, and he didn't relinquish my hand once I was on dry land, but instead raised it to his lips, heedless of a skein of green weed sticking to my knuckles. "This is an honour. What do water nymphs drink, by the way?"

Nobody had ever kissed my hand before. I was too fascinated by the gesture to answer immediately, watching the way his full lips touched my skin and his eyes lifted to mine.

"We like coffee," I hazarded, though I thought it unlikely.

"That's lucky. I have a pot right over there, on that table. Let's go and sit down, shall we?"

He led me, still in possession of my hand, up the sloping bank to a flat expanse of lawn where a wrought iron table and chairs stood beneath a lime tree, set for a late breakfast with coffee, a basket of pastries and a folded newspaper.

"I think," he said, pulling out a chair for me, "that you are not a German naiad. Am I right? Perhaps American? British?"

"We're fairly international," I said, not wanting to think about who or what I was. I didn't want to answer any personal questions, unless it was, "Would you like to go to bed with me?" I couldn't help knowing that the answer to that would be, "Yes."

"I suppose you are," he said, pouring the coffee. "Do you take it with cream?"

I nodded. I couldn't help appreciating the fact that he had, as yet, made absolutely no reference to my nudity. This could be any polite morning meeting between friends or colleagues. Or lovers.

He pushed the cup over to me, leaving himself without.

"Oh," I said, feeling guilty about this. "But I've taken your cup."

He waved his hand.

"You are my special guest," he said. "Besides, I already had one. Would you prefer it if we spoke English? I am fluent and would appreciate the opportunity to practise."

How long had it been since I'd met a man with such ridiculously good manners? I really couldn't remember but I was captivated.

"If you like," I said, in English. "I don't mind. My German is pretty good, considering."

"Oh yes, it is excellent, I didn't mean to imply otherwise," he said, also in English. Damn him, now he was even sexier, speaking with that accent. He had the sort of voice that soaks into you and makes you crave more of it. I would have been perfectly happy to sit there sipping coffee and listening to him talk indefinitely.

He cocked his head to one side and appraised me in a way that made me feel the flush all over my body. My nipples tightened. He must have noticed.

"You must think me extremely rude," he said, and my whole body did a kind of jolt, as if electrified, resulting in an incredulous little laugh. Why on earth would I think that? Did he know that 'rude' could be construed in another way? The emphasis he placed on it, together with a little glint at the corner of his eyes, suggested that he did.

"Rude? No, not at all. Why?"

"I haven't introduced myself. Forgive me. I am Johannes Eberhardt, of Eberhardt Technologies. I don't expect you have heard of it."

"Oh ... vaguely, perhaps. And I am ..." I didn't want to say it. It was absurd, but I clung stubbornly to my alter ego. "Flosshilde."

He laughed, but I thought he was slightly stung by my failure to reciprocate with honesty.

"Then you *are* a Rhinemaiden," he remarked. "Albeit one who may have gotten herself lost in the Thames." He paused and his gaze intensified. "Tell me, Flosshilde, what is it like to live in water?"

"It's ... good," I said, unsure of where we were going with this. "You feel light and free. The water holds you and keeps you safe from the dangers on land."

"Are there no dangers in the water?"

"Dangers?"

"Predators," he said, and I swear the way he said it made me clench. It was a statement of intent.

"I, uh, I'm not sure." My breath had stopped.

"Surely there must be all kinds of creatures pursuing such a beautiful body, wanting to take it and make it their own?"

OK. We had taken a roundabout route to get there, but now we were definitely hovering around the gateway to sex. Was I all right with it?

Yes.

"They try," I said, annoyed with myself at how the words came out, all sticky and breathy with obvious desire. "But none of them have caught me yet."

"Not while you are in your element," he said. "But now you are out of it."

"Yes," I said, fixing my eyes on his as boldly as I could. "I am, a bit."

"The dangers of land," he quoted me, with a dazzling smile. "Terrible dangers. Let me show you."

He picked up one of the pastries from the basket and broke off a crumbly, buttery section. He held it to my lips, leaning across the table.

"Take it," he said softly. "Even naiads need to eat,

yes?"

I let him feed me, and when his fingertips lingered about my lips, I licked the crumbs from them. I couldn't seem to stop myself, and he was delighted to see it.

"So this little water sprite," he said, brushing my collarbone clean, "has let herself be caught and brought to land. Isn't she afraid?"

I half-shook my head, but I wanted to nod at the same time. Yes, I was. No, I wasn't.

"I'll tell you what," he said. "I'm a generous man. I'll give you a chance."

"Oh?"

"You can finish your coffee and then you can choose where to go. Into the water, where I can't catch you, or into the house, where I can."

I caught my breath. "Right." My choice was already made, not that I would have told him.

"And while you're thinking about that," he said, "is there anybody who might miss you? Anybody you want to call? Because it's only fair to mention that, if I catch you, I mean to keep you—at least all day long and perhaps longer. But that will depend on you, I guess."

He took a mobile phone from his inner jacket pocket and pushed it across the table to me.

Did I want to tell anyone where I was? Would anybody care? Would Louis even notice? And if I texted somebody now, would this man, this Johannes Eberhardt, take that as a capitulation from me? I was rather looking forward to a chase now …

"You know," I said, pushing it back, "I don't think I do. Not yet."

He pushed it towards me again.

"No," he said, quite seriously this time. "At least text somebody, tell them where you are and with whom. I know you're a naiad and you might not understand modern mores, but perhaps you should learn."

Oh dear. He was telling me off. And it was turning me on.

I took the phone and sent a brief text message, not to Louis but to Julia.

"Am next door with rich bloke. See u l8r."

What a weird message. She was bound to try and call me back. Hopefully he would switch off his phone when we … if we …

Oh god. *Don't break the spell. Just go with it.*

"You must think I'm terrible," I blurted, the text message having brought an unwelcome note of reality into proceedings.

"No," he said gently, his eyes … how did he *do* that with his eyes? I trembled beneath them. "I don't think that at all. If I thought that, I wouldn't be sitting here thinking about all the things I'd like to do to you."

Do them to me.

"If you catch me," I said.

"Ah yes. If I catch you. Are you finished?"

He looked down at the coffee, which I had drunk to the dregs.

"I have," I said, pushing back my chair with legs that were maddeningly weak. I had to peel myself off the chair and I imagined the pattern of wrought-iron curls stamped into my bottom and thighs. What a sight for him, along with the lakeweed.

"Oh, that's right, it should be 'have you finished'," he said, sounding rather sweetly crestfallen to be caught out in grammatical inaccuracy. "I'm sorry."

"It's OK. You can say 'are' as well, but it's more American English than British English. So it's fine."

"I spend more time in the States than the UK, you see," he said. "I am more in tune with their rhythms of speech."

"Your English is bloody amazing," I consoled him. "Don't sweat it, as they might say over there."

"Thank you," he said, brightening. "I like to be accurate, that's all. But you have a decision to make, I think? Will it be the lake?" He waved one hand in an elegant flourish. "Or will it be the house?"

His eyes told me that he knew the answer, but I made a couple of false steps in the other direction first, just to tease, before turning and fleeing across the lawn.

Now he would see my patterned rear, but I didn't care. I didn't care about anything except the breeze between my thighs and in my hair and the soft grass underfoot and the feeling of sheer freedom my nakedness gave me. I was restrained by nothing, constrained by nothing, and only the sun could see me. Only the sun and Herr Eberhardt ...

The house careened towards me, its wedding-cake yellow and whiteness filling up my sights. I risked a quick glance over my shoulder, but Herr Eberhardt had not even risen from his chair yet. In fact, he was reading the newspaper.

I laughed to myself at his sheer effrontery and allowed myself to slow down. He was very sure he would catch me. Well, I wouldn't make it *that* easy for him.

I found a pair of open French doors and strolled through them on to cool, dark wood flooring. It certainly showed up our shabby bolthole next door for what it was ... this was a rich person's house, all right. I took a little time to examine the tasteful furnishings and run my fingers along the keys of a baby grand piano.

I could never resist a bookshelf and I wondered if Herr Eberhardt had read all these tomes or they were just for display. Goethe's *Werther*, on which I'd written my dissertation, was there in a splendid blue and gold livery. I wanted to take it out and flick through it ... but perhaps I should leave it for later.

Should I go upstairs or down? Upstairs seemed a bad plan. Much more difficult to get away from, plus bedrooms … I went down a spiral stair into a dark panelled corridor. I pushed open a door and clapped my hands.

There was an indoor pool, not Olympic sized by any means, but big enough for a good splash about. And a jacuzzi. And …

I stood underneath the poolside shower, washing off the lakeweed and the residual sunbaked grime. The pressure was deliciously strong, pelting on to my skin like a brisk massage. When it started to hurt my nipples, I stepped aside, wondering if Herr Eberhardt had finished reading the share price index yet, or whatever he was into.

What *was* he … into …?

For the first time it occurred to me to be nervous. This man was an unknown quantity and, what was more, he was a rich unknown quantity residing in an isolated place. Perhaps he was one of those elite men with 'specialist tastes' that fell well outside the normal, or even legal, spectrum. Shit!

But then I remembered his insistence on my sending a text with my whereabouts and felt reassured. But then, perhaps if he was rich enough and powerful enough …

I thought about escaping in earnest. It was probably the sane thing to do.

I switched off the shower and went to the door,

but before I could even decide what I was doing, I heard footsteps on the floor overhead and I ducked back behind the door, breathing hard, a big fluffy towel clutched to my breasts.

He was coming down the stairs.

My first instinct was to dive into the pool, but I would be completely visible there. There was a wooden door, kind of a stable door, at the far end of the room, but it was no guarantee of a way out.

I ran instead to the jacuzzi and climbed hastily into its bubbling depths. If I could lurk in here until he came close, then duck underneath and hold my breath for long enough, perhaps he might not see me beneath the chaotic foam of the surface.

Not that I even wanted to elude capture, but it seemed important that I play the game properly—to me and, I was pretty sure, to him as well.

I knelt in the maelstrom, keeping my head down, trying not to giggle at the way the jets pounded against my body, especially my inner thighs and breasts.

Seconds later, the door was pushed lightly open and I could almost feel his presence radiating towards me. What if he could feel mine? That would be weird and yet it seemed possible.

"I think you are in here," he said. "It seems the obvious place for a naiad to come to."

Damn, he was right. Totally obvious. I had

unconsciously sought out the water without any reference to what might be unexpected.

I thought about just giving myself up then and there. I didn't realistically expect to be able to escape him. His footsteps tapped, echoing, on the tiled floor. They were slow and deliberate. He was not a man to ever be rushed.

I hugged my arms around my knees and bent lower, my shoulders cresting the roiling waters. Only my head was now above them.

"You can't hide forever," he said in a sinister sing-song. "I am going to catch you."

I inhaled as quietly and deeply as I could and stuck my head in the water.

I didn't hear his next words, though they came from somewhere quite close. An impression of his voice mingled with the roar of the jets, all of it fragmenting inside my head. How long before I could come up for air?

He seemed to go silent just before my lungs threatened to burst.

I broke the surface of the water again, gasping so hard that it was a moment or two before I registered his face, peering down at me from above arms that were folded on top of the tiled wall of the jacuzzi.

An indulgent smile played about his lips.

"Damn," I panted.

"Nice try," he said. "But I could see your hair." He

stood straight. "And now I have a naiad of my very own. No, stay there."

I had thought to climb out and hand myself over, but he was unbuttoning his shirt. Apparently he meant to join me.

I watched, mesmerised by his deft fingers at the buttons, then by his toned chest. I looked for silver hairs, but there were none, although he was greying at the temples. To all intents and purposes, this was the chest of a man in peak physical condition.

I could say the same for his stomach, and then his legs when he removed his trousers. He folded them neatly, took off his heavy-looking watch, then I waited expectantly for his next trick. Only a pair of grey silk boxers remained.

"I thought you would be more comfortable," he said, hooking his thumbs in the waistband, "if we both were naked."

"Oh," I said. "That's thoughtful of you."

"Yes," he said. "I try." He took off the boxers and I looked away, a little flustered.

There was a plunge, a displacement of water, and then he was beside me, sitting on the little ledge seat and pulling me towards him.

His hand around my upper arm felt good, as did the tiny but inescapable amount of pressure he exerted in bringing me to his side.

"Now," he said, his arm around my shoulder, his lips close to mine. "I had forgotten how it felt to sit in here. It's quite stimulating, don't you think?"

"Those jets are powerful," I agreed, drawn into his orbit, feeling every iota of his desire for me as if it soaked into my skin with the water.

"It's just the right place to spend time with my captive naiad," he said. "But I don't mean to ignore your wishes. What would you like to do?"

"I'm … good … here," I said, overcome by a sense of intoxication that sent my mind reeling. His lips were so almost, so virtually, on mine. I could feel his breath and I could feel his skin and I wanted to press deeper into the embrace of his arm around me.

"Oh yes? You like it here? So perhaps," he said, putting a finger between our mouths and running along my lower lip, "I could build a cage over the top of this jacuzzi and keep you here always?"

I had nothing to say to that. But my lips gave him an answer nonetheless, in the quiver of my breath, followed by their grateful surrender to the longed-for kiss. He exerted the perfect level of pressure, not too hard, not too soft. He took my will from me in that kiss and sucked it into him. Now it was his.

He broke it just as my stomach was roiling in a decent imitation of the jacuzzi jets and I thought he would say something sweet or gentlemanly, as befitted my experience of him.

So it was a shock when he rasped, "Get your ass on my lap, now."

He pulled me up to sit with my bare bottom on his thighs and held me tight before plunging into another kiss. This one was deeper, profound and searching, and it introduced his tongue to mine. They twisted together like seaweed fronds, but with more purpose.

I was still reacting to his outburst, wondering whether or not it was uncharacteristic. I was not averse to a man giving orders in the bedroom—although I'd never encountered anything like it before. It was strange and slightly alarming to hear it like that, though, without a softening 'please'. How did he know I wouldn't tell him to get lost? But of course, it was obvious. It was what I was there for and he knew it.

I was pierced by a little spike of shame, but rather than giving me pause it spurred me on, making me want to be dirtier and more wanton than ever. This man knew and understood me. He wasn't wrong about me. I did want to be taken and used and owned and kept captive by him. For now, anyway.

I squirmed in his lap, enjoying the way the bubbles forced themselves up between the junctions of our bodies. I enjoyed even more his hands' eager efforts to chart every inch of my skin. They glided everywhere, up my arms, down my spine, around my hips. Soon they held my breasts, squeezing them, circling my nipples as if measuring their diameter. Then he reached down, cupping my buttocks, pinching them with firm, sure fingers. He maintained the kiss with ferocious intent all along, until I lay limp and half-insensate from the constant bombardment of stimulation.

"Flosshilde," he said at last, and I was confused until I remembered that was the name I'd given him. "Do you think humans and naiads can fuck?"

"I'm pretty sure," I said, gasping for breath. "I think so."

He moved to stand, bucking my expectations yet again—he seemed to like doing this.

"Oh," I said.

He climbed out of the jacuzzi and offered a hand to help me follow him.

"Humans and naiads might not be sexually incompatible," he said, smiling at my bewilderment. "But who knows what might happen if they reproduce? And I don't keep any prophylactics down here."

"Oh, right." I felt stupid, my cheeks burning. My lust for him seemed to have killed off a few of my brain cells. Why did it have to do that?

He kissed me.

"Go and lie down on the lawn," he said.

Another bucking of my expectations, and a strange one at that.

"Lie down … on the lawn?" I echoed. "You mean … outside?"

"I do mean outside," he said with a devastating smile. "Where else do I have a lawn?"

"Just … lie down on it?"

"That's right. In the shade would be best. I don't want you to burn." He reached around and gave my bottom a sharp tap. The sound of it echoed around the underground chamber. "Go on then. And don't think of running away. You're mine now, remember."

I wasn't likely to forget. I followed him up the stairs, looking after him when he waved me through the double doors out to the garden. He had gone to rummage in a locked drawer.

And now here I was, walking dripping and naked across a neat sloping lawn towards a lime tree. If anyone was out on the lake, they would be able to see me, but there were no boats. Even mine was no longer visible, having probably drifted out past the weeping willows at the edge of Eberhardt's land. I was going to find a spot to lie down and be ravished upon.

The knowledge of this was intense and focused my mind even more than my bare, wet skin and the soft summer breeze upon it.

I walked willingly to the scene of my shame. I knew he would fuck me, and he knew I knew, and he knew I wanted it. The awareness of it was both liberating and shocking. And he had chosen for it to happen in the open air, potentially in view of lake-borne vessels. He had no intention of sparing me a single blush.

I arrived in the shade of the lime tree and sat down, shivering a little. It wasn't cold, but the shade gave me a tiny sensation of chill, goose-pimpling my skin. Or perhaps that was nerves. I wrapped my arms around my knees and hugged them against my breasts, squashing my stiff nipples. They were beginning to ache from being so swollen for so long. He had touched them, pressed them, they were his now.

What would it be like to be his, in reality? To live here in his lakeside house, subject to his will? I drifted into a fantasy life, imagining us sitting in a boat at sunset while he fed me strawberries, talking about what he would do to me when he got me home to bed. I'd like to hear him talk like that, hear him say those words.

He'd keep me in a shallow pool, chained to the side because naiads were notoriously slippery creatures who could not be trusted. He'd unchain me when he wanted to take me out of my element and use me. He'd use me a lot …

I was shaken out of my increasingly lurid imaginings by his voice, making me jump.

"I thought I told you to lie down."

It was light, pleasantly-spoken, but I knew at once that I should do as he said. Only somebody completely deaf to nuance could have failed the recognise the steel beneath the smile.

He was carrying things. Not just condoms. A cool box of the kind you'd use for a picnic, and a watering can. How strange.

But I didn't question it. I straightened my spine down among the daisies and felt the cool tickle of the grass between my thighs. Above me, the sun glinted and hid through a tangle of branch and leaf. I could fall asleep like this, if only it weren't for the face, looking down at me from a height, sweeping my prostrate form with hungry but pitiless eyes.

"How do you feel, Naiad?" he asked.

He had put down his burden and tightened the belt of his silk robe around him. He hadn't offered one of those to me. I could do with one. The breeze was becoming more evident, especially around my nipples.

"I feel vulnerable," I said, pressing my thighs together and curling my toes.

"Vulnerable, yes, good. But are you comfortable?"

"I think so."

"Not too dry? Poor little naiad is used to the water, isn't she?"

"I suppose so." The residual drops from the jacuzzi had all slid off my skin now.

He knelt down by my side and passed his hands

over my upper torso, rubbing and stroking over my breasts
and collarbone and down over my stomach.

"Yes, I think so," he said, bending to kiss my navel.
"Very dry. This must not be comfortable for you?"

"It's …"

But before I could continue, I let out a sharp cry.

He had reached into his picnic box and brought
something out, which he placed square on my belly. It was
a goddamn ice cube!

"Oh my *god*, that's *freezing*!"

I tried to turn so it would slide off, but he tutted
and held it in place with the tip of a finger.

"No, no, no," he said. "This is good for you."

I wriggled and shivered and whimpered while he
sent the cube on a little journey, leaving cold wet tracks
across my skin. He let it glide between my breasts, then
climb their slopes, circling—but never quite coming into
contact with—my nipples, until the damn thing melted.

I was gasping with the cold, but he showed mercy
by kissing all the places the cube had chilled, warming
them back up with his fulsome lips and tongue.

I wondered if he could tell that I was ready for him
now … more than ready. My clit felt ready to burst with
need for his attention and I didn't need any ice cube to get
me wet down there. Could he scent it? Something told me
that he could.

But it didn't mean he was going to go easy on me.

Another bullet of ice materialised on my nipple, making me arch my spine and howl. He was amused by this, holding my poor throbbing bud between finger and thumb and keeping the ice cube where he wanted it. He kept it there, not moving, just until my nipple went beyond pain and into numbness, then he transferred it to the other. The expression of satisfaction on his face told me how he enjoyed watching me writhe. I didn't find it frightening. I found it intensely arousing. He was using me the way he wanted and I was willing to comply, even if it did mean purple nipples.

"I know it's cold," he whispered. "But you'll warm it up, won't you? Because you aren't cold. You're on fire."

He put his free hand between my thighs and rubbed the juicy swollen clit he found there. Yes, there was his proof. I couldn't deny what I was, what I craved.

The ice shrunk and disappeared, its existence only evidenced by the rivulets trickling down my breasts into the furrow between them.

Eberhardt put his face there and lapped up the crystal droplets, then flicked the tip of his tongue over my recovering nipples. The warmth buzzed them back into painful life. I wriggled my bottom into the buttercups as he opened his lips and sucked.

He alternated between nipples, dipping lazy fingers between my pussy lips and into my cunt at the same time.

I was so close to coming from the double stimulation of being fingered and sucked simultaneously that I began to squirm. Instantly, he stopped what he was doing and smiled down at me. The sun had gone in. The leaves rustled against a stronger breath of wind.

"Oh," was all I could whisper.

"Not yet," he teased. "Naiads are very sensual little creatures, aren't they? I had no idea. I think more ice ..."

"Oh no," I moaned, but he was quick and deft and before I could clamp my legs together he was holding a cube to my clit. I kicked my legs against the acuteness of the sensation, but he rubbed slowly, up and down, then in slow circles, using his free hand to stroke and brush and pinch my nipples. I cried out and he popped a finger in my mouth, silencing me, making me suck on it. Now all I could do was hump my bottom up and down in a useless quest to free myself from my freezing invader.

"This is good," he crooned. "You are doing well." He pushed the cube inside me, where it melted almost straight away. I felt the cold fluid mingle with my own warm juices and trickle between my butt cheeks. I had never felt ruder, more ashamed or more turned on.

"Lovely," he said, shifting position and taking his finger from my mouth.

"Oh, please, not another," I pleaded, panting.

He climbed in between my knees and bent his head to my vulva, his eyes devilish as they peered up from my pubic mound.

"You don't like it?" he asked, his breath blasting my clit as he spoke.

"It's ... torture," I said.

He clicked his tongue. "Awww." The expression of exaggerated sympathy ended with a little kiss on my clit. "Cold," he commented.

"Uh, yeah," I said, but sarcasm probably wasn't in order just now, when there was every chance of getting a dozen ice cubes tipped over my defenceless body.

He raised his head again, along with a finger which he wagged at me.

"You said please and asked me very nicely before, and that's the only reason I'm not reaching for another ice cube right now. But I can change my mind at any moment."

So I was to behave myself. I wanted to behave myself. This strict teacher vibe he was projecting really worked for me.

I nodded and tried to look doe-eyed.

He seemed satisfied with that, but he had more to say.

"What you have to understand, Flosshilde, is that you belong to me now. I don't think any of your little water sprite friends are going to swim up to the bank to rescue you, do you?"

"I guess not."

"You're lucky that you've been captured by a reasonable man. A lot of those men on the other side of the lake are a lot less reasonable than I am. They are cruel to their naiads. They beat them and tie them up and humiliate them. I'm not going to do that to you ... unless you ask for it." He smirked briefly and his eyelid hovered on the verge of a wink before correcting itself.

Oh yes? I thought, perking up. *Kinky as hell, aren't you, mein Herr, and this is your way of putting the onus on me to show my hand.*

Well, it was clever. It made me crush on him even more.

He waited for me to speak, but I didn't, so he continued.

"But if you behave yourself," he said, "I will be good to you. I will treat you well. I will give you whatever you ask ... except your freedom."

It was like an exquisite game. I was too exhilarated and too caught up in my pleasurable game-fear of him to say anything. I just wanted to know what he was going to do next.

"Do you understand?" he said softly, making it clear that an answer was required of me.

"Yes," I whispered, and I added, irresistibly, without even thinking, "sir."

"I think I need to test your understanding," he said, although I could see from the way his eyes had lit that he really liked the 'sir'. "Sit up."

I struggled up on my elbows and sat facing him, still with my thighs wide apart and him kneeling between them. We were very close. My nipples brushed the silk of his robe.

"Put your hands on your head," he commanded, and I obeyed straight away, trying not to laugh at how strange it felt, and how nervous I suddenly was.

"Good. Now I am going to go inside for a little while, and I want you to stay exactly as you are, without moving a muscle."

I let out a little huff of disappointment at his going away again; my ice-cube-tormented body was on high alert, desperate for his touch.

He reached over to the picnic bag again and I tensed, wondering if another ordeal by ice was part of the test. But instead, he brought out a delicious looking fruit tart topped with an extravagant swirl of whipped cream and laid it on paper plate between my legs.

I looked up at him with curiosity.

"That is your test," he said, standing up. "If the cake has moved, I know that you have moved." He patted my thighs together and put the plate on top of them where it sat, a mite lopsidedly, just below my pubic triangle. "If it remains there, completely intact, I know that you have done as you were told. What happens to you next depends on that cake."

"Does it?" I asked with a thrill of fear.

"If I find it as I left it, you can have it to eat. If I don't, then I am afraid I will have to punish you."

"What sort of punishment?"

"Ah, you are thinking of disobeying me, or you wouldn't ask. Oh dear." He bent and tapped my cheek, smiling devilishly right into my face. "What a pity that would be. But don't worry. It wouldn't be too painful. Just enough to make you think."

Oh god. I could hardly breathe. I watched him turn and walk away towards the house and all I could think of was how much I suddenly and definitely wanted to explore my hidden kinks. I had them all right. I'd read enough books about men with whips and the defenceless women who grew, after some initial discomfort, to adore them. But I'd never, ever dreamed that I'd get the chance to experience it in real life. I mean, how did one ever bring the subject up without risking making a giant fool of oneself? It just hadn't been worth the potential humiliation.

Humiliation.

I looked down at the cake, lying on my thighs, mocking me.

Eberhardt went inside the house without looking back. I had no idea how long he would be in there, nor what he would do to me when he came out. I sat there, hands on head, my nipples and pussy warming up after their encounter with the ice cubes, looking out to the balmy lake.

Again, he was giving me a chance to go, to swim away, to put this behind me.

I could do that.

Or I could eat the cake.

I ate the cake.

I almost didn't. I unclasped my fingers and clasped them again half a dozen times while the paper plate juddered perilously on my lap.

Then, with a move so swift half the cream fell in a gloopy mess on my thigh, I picked the damn thing up and took a good bite.

Sweet crumbly pastry, thick confectioner's custard and half a glazed strawberry melted together in my mouth. God, the Germans knew about cake. You had to hand it to them. *The Great Mittel-European Bake-Off* would be something to watch. The Austrians and Hungarians would give them a good run for their money though.

Whatever fate Eberhardt had in store for me, this mouthgasm was worth it.

Or so I thought. Until I'd swallowed every last morsel and all that was left was the blob of cream, sinking into the skin of my thigh and beginning to run down the side and drip on the grass.

The cake was gone and I was done for. I put the paper plate aside and dipped a finger into the thinning cream. I couldn't wait to find out what was going to happen to me and I kept looking up at the house, but there was no flicker of movement from its many arched windows.

It seemed a bit pointless to put my hands back on my head, given the act of gross insubordination I'd just committed, but I did it anyway. A half-measure might be better than nothing.

But what was he going to *do* to me?

My eyes drifted over to the cool box, the pack of condoms—still unused—and the watering can. Also still unused. What was it all *for?*

I was still theorising when some sixth sense told me he was in the air. I looked sharply over to the French doors and saw him coming out, fully dressed again in a pale linen suit and blue chalk-stripe open-necked shirt, with a bag slung across his shoulder, some kind of satchel thing. What was in it?

He had already seen that the cake was gone, and he increased his pace, striding quickly across the lawn with an expression that worked hard to try and disguise how secretly pleased he was about it.

"You naiads have healthy appetites," he hailed me, when he was close enough to be heard. "But I thought we had an agreement. Didn't we?"

I chewed my lip, words failing me.

"Was it delicious?" he asked, kneeling beside me with a vulpine smile. "Oh, but you haven't finished."

He dipped a finger in the runny cream, scooping it up my thigh, then placed it at my lips.

"It was very delicious," I said, licking the cream from his fingertip.

"But you don't like cream?"

"I love cream."

His smile, if possible, widened even further. I could see every tooth in his head.

"That's lucky," he said. He scooped up the rest and sucked it from his own finger. "Mm. Yes. But that's where your luck runs out, my dear, because I think you must remember the conversation we had earlier? Hmm?"

I nodded, my eyes sliding sideways.

"Remind me," he whispered. "What did I say?"

"You said I had to stay in position and not eat the cake."

"Right. And what did I say would happen if you ate the cake?"

I couldn't get the words out.

"Something bad," I muttered.

He tutted and tapped underneath my chin with one fingertip, forcing me to look him in the eyes.

"I need you to be more specific, *Schatzi*."

The German term of endearment liquefied me. I was powerless to resist him.

"You said you would ..."

"Go on." He stroked the tender skin beneath my jawbone as if coaxing out the words.

"Punish me."

The words sounded foreign, although I thought I would have found them easier to say in German. The Rammstein song *Bestrafe Mich* barged into my head, almost making me giggle.

"Yes, I did. And what did you do?"

"I ... ate the cake."

"You ate the cake. So what happens now?"

"I suppose ... you're going to punish me?"

He smiled again, almost regretfully, and patted my cheek.

"That's right," he said. "My naiad has to learn. Now, is your leg clean? Is it sticky? I'm thinking of my suit. I don't want to ruin it."

He reached into his bag and took out a pack of wet wipes, dabbing at my thigh until all residual traces of my guilt were gone.

"What are you going to do to me?" I asked. I was scared, I think, but it was such a heady, exhilarating kind of fear that I couldn't really distinguish it from excitement.

"What do you think I should do to you?"

Oh, now, this wasn't fair.

I cocked my head to one side in an attempt at

coquetry, though this wasn't really my style as a rule.

"Forgive me," I suggested.

He laughed.

"Oh, I will forgive you. I never bear grudges. But you must be punished, and punished you will be. Come on."

He took my hand and pulled me to my feet.

"Where are we going?" I asked, but I hadn't even finished the sentence before we arrived at a wide tree stump a few yards behind the lime.

He put down his bag, sat, and patted his thigh.

I had seen this gesture often in my bedtime imaginings, but never thought I would see it in reality. I knew exactly what it meant, but I was still tempted to act the wide-eyed naïf.

My hesitation earned me raised eyebrows and another pointed slap of his thigh. I couldn't get away with pretending.

"Do you mean …?" I stammered.

"You know what to do, I am sure," he said. "But just so there is no room for misinterpretation or accusations after the event, I'll make it clear. I am going to spank you on your bottom until it is bright red. Is that clear enough or should I say more?"

"I, um, that's clear enough," I said, in a fever of internal squirming.

"If it is too much for you, you can stop me by saying … oh, I don't know …"

I'd heard of safe words. I thought I ought to come up with one of my own, in case he decided on one of those endless German portmanteau words. *Geschwindingkeitsbeschränkung* or *Rechtsschutzversicherungsgesellschaften* would not trip off the tongue in the midst of my travails.

"Faust," I said.

He stared at me and then barked with laughter.

"I like that. OK, I'm waiting."

He projected such an aura of calm authority that it seemed unthinkable to disobey now. I felt grateful for it as I draped myself across his lap—grateful that I did not have to giggle or make self-conscious jokey remarks or stiffen with discomfort at the situation. He made it easy for me to slip into that most dissonant of all mindsets— submissiveness.

I tried to analyse and capture how it felt, to be bent over this man's knee for a spanking. It didn't feel the way I'd imagined it might. I wasn't crippled with shame and embarrassment for a start—they had been overlaid with curiosity and excitement and a mild hope that it wouldn't be too painful. I wanted to see this through, to know where it would lead.

"You have not behaved well," he said sternly, and his voice brought that sense of shame that had been eluding me flooding in. "You were told not to touch the cake—and you ate it. So you know that you deserve this, don't you?"

"Yes," I said meekly.

"Yes," he said, with a sudden and breathtaking smack on one of my bare bottom cheeks. "Sir." Another. "Say it properly."

"Yes, sir," I yelped out without hesitation.

"Better. I wish I didn't have to do this ..." He left a pause long enough to insert my own mental accusation of fibbing. "But you must learn. You are in my care and you must stick to my rules. Now push that bottom up higher."

This entailed tensing my thighs to an uncomfortable degree, but I was keen to show my eagerness, so I did it.

He delivered the spanking with such amazing skill that it never crossed the border into real pain, whilst still seeming like a punishment. I don't know how he did it— perhaps it was the mild scolding that accompanied his rhythmic attack on my posterior. It was something to do with his voice, anyway, or perhaps the words he spoke, or the way he made the smacks ring out so that the ducks at the edge of the lake were ruffled and flew away, quacking their indignation.

"You have to understand," he said, his words oozing into my ears and mixing into the haze of lust that had taken me over, "that you cannot do just what you like here. It is my house, and you abide by my rules. Even if you think those rules are silly." He reached into his bag at this point and took something out. I found out what it was when it made contact with my bottom—it was some kind of leather paddle. Perhaps his hand was sore, I thought. "Lots of my rules are silly, I admit that to you."

Ouch! The paddle hurt, but it also felt amazingly good while the leather was still cold on my heated skin. And I was beyond caring about nonsense like pain now. I was swimming in it, just as I would in the water. I was part of it now, and it was part of me.

"For instance," he continued in his soft yet unerringly firm tones, "it is not a very practical rule that you have to be naked all the time when I am in the house. You might say that was a silly rule. But I require you to keep it."

I sucked in a breath and began to waggle my feet, the burn of the paddle spreading down low into my deep tissues.

"And I have a rule that you have to beg me for your orgasm. I will nearly always say yes. But you must beg me, very humbly, first."

I twisted my spine. It was a real effort now to take the continuing volley of hard strokes but I couldn't bear to use my safe word. And I wanted to hear some more of these bizarre but arousing rules.

"And I also have a rule," he continued, the paddle falling very fast and very hard now, "that you use your safe word when you have to instead of trying to impress me." He threw the paddle aside and pulled my hair hard until my head was angled back to meet his eyes. "Hmm?"

Oh dear, I was so busted. How was I to know that he could read minds? Or bottoms?

"I didn't need to," I said. "Honestly. But it was getting close."

"I know. But thank you."

He smiled, the crinkles around his eyes making them lighten somehow.

"It is rather sweet," he said, letting go of my hair and stroking it. "Very."

His other hand cupped my burning bottom and rubbed it. The effect was both soothing and inflaming. I could have lain there all day, just as long as he let his fingers wander lower …

But instead he gave my bottom a final smack and said, "Now that is dealt with, I want you back under the tree on all fours. Now, please."

I arranged myself beside the watering can, still wondering what it was for.

I soon found out.

Eberhardt circled me for a while, looking at me from every angle, stopping every now and then to stroke his chin and stare as if making mental calculations. It was unnerving, but I was starting to relish the loss of nerve now. It always seemed to presage some experience of new and unimaginable pleasure. For reasons I couldn't begin to explain, I trusted him.

Eventually he came behind me and I saw his jacket tossed to the base of the tree, then I heard him unbuckle his belt. My pussy quivered and my pelvic floor contracted, knowing what was coming next.

I wanted it so much, really wanted to have this man inside me, connected to me, joined with me. I wanted to be his. I wanted, in that moment, for the whole captive naiad thing to be really true and for me to be his treasured possession instead of his casual sex partner. I held the fantasy still in my head and refused to let it go, keeping it there during the snap of rubber and the clap of his hand on my shoulder, then another on my hip, then the nudge of his cock at my opening.

I belong to you. You take me. I am yours.

I was so deep in this fantasy that the first drop of warmish water between my shoulder blades took me by surprise. I nearly jolted him off, but he held me by my hip and continued to ease inside me, inch by inch, while a stream flowed down my spine and off my sides.

"What …?" I breathed.

"Don't you understand?" he said, pushing himself in to the hilt and letting more water fall on my neck, then my still very warm bottom. "You need the water. You need to be wet." He emptied the whole of the watering can over me, then cupped my breasts with wet hands, making sure I was completely drenched all over.

Only then could he begin to thrust, slowly at first, kissing the knobs of my damp spine, kissing all the hollows where it had pooled, licking it up on the tip of his tongue while he fucked me with steadily gathering force. I was hot, cold, wet and utterly wild for him, pushing back on him, wanting him to do it harder, harder, harder.

He did as well, mounting to a pace that made me gasp and grunt and feel his pelvis smacking my sore bottom all over again, reawakening that precious sting. Water lay in beads on my tight, hot skin. I imagined it melting into steam, rising off me, forming a fog that would be visible from the lake.

He put one finger on my clit and worked at it. I felt my eyes rolling, my sense uncoupling from my senses. The steam was thickening. My pussy was wetter than it had ever been, and it was nothing to do with the water. I could hear how slick I was, his cock stretching me, making a sucking noise with every thrust. I was getting close. I was drowning in the steam. I was stretched and held and fucked and owned and …

A memory. Something he said.

"Please," I gasped. "Oh please, let me …"

"Are you going to come?"

His lips were at my ear, his voice a gentle wave, lapping over my head.

"Mm, yes, please, yes."

"You may." His cheek was against mine as I

wriggled and squirmed and sighed into orgasm. He fucked me through it, his mouth at my ear, whispering things in German that I was too far gone to translate. The last one was harsh and sudden and he pressed his fingertips hard into me while he said it. He held himself still, then loosened, exhaling a long tickling breath on to my neck.

We rolled over on to our backs and lay like that, in each other's arms, until we dried off and the sun passed high over us and began to lower.

"You know, I really would like to keep you," he said, startling me out of sleep.

"What?"

"I would like a captive naiad. To keep," he clarified. "But you will go home and pick up your real life and this will all be a strange thing that happened on a hot day when you were younger. A dream."

"I'm not really a naiad," I said. "But if you want to keep me, you can. I mean, not forever. But for a bit longer. Until we've had enough, maybe."

He turned his head, his lips twitching towards a smile.

"Until we've had enough," he repeated. "OK. Why not? Why don't you start by telling me your name."

Hard to Swallow

◆◆◆◆

By

Lisette Ashton

Hard to Swallow

◆◆◆◆

"Ten points to me," called Tony.

Addison sat behind the reception desk. She was striving to ignore his exclamation whilst she attempted to look like a model of efficiency. Wearing a short dark skirt and a blouse the same liquid blue as the radio station's corporate logo, she knew she fitted in with the über-sleek stylings of her glamorous glass-and-steel surroundings. But this was still her first day, and Addison worried that everyone passing by the desk would see she was merely a wannabe presenter. She worried that everyone would know she had only assumed the thinly-veiled pretence of being a receptionist so she could be on hand should an emergency-presenter-vacancy arise in one of the station's many studios.

It was a long-shot, she supposed.

But Addison was nothing if not optimistic.

She knew the odds of winning the lottery were millions-to-one against, but she had seen enough lottery winners on the news to know they existed. Consequently, whilst she knew the chances of her being called from the reception desk to a recording studio were incredibly thin, she also realised that just being in the building meant that a chance for such an opportunity did exist.

It was a hopeful thought that always made her smile. More importantly, it distracted her from the monotony of working alongside Tony.

Tony was supposedly showing her how to work on the reception desk.

He was five years her senior and since Stern, the station manager, had assigned him the role of showing Addison how to fulfil her duties, he hadn't stopped trying to entertain her with inane chatter, engage her with 'interesting' facts or amuse her with senseless diversions.

It had been a long day.

She suspected Tony was trying to hit on her. As much as she appreciated his efforts to help fight the boredom, Addison had already come to the conclusion that a terminal dose of ennui would be preferable to Tony's desperate attempts at workplace fun.

Tony pointed at a presenter walking through the reception's main doors.

She was a tall, elegant brunette with a cell phone pressed against one ear. She wore cranberry chinos beneath a white blouse under a vintage little black Chanel jacket. There was a dark green bottle of mineral water in her left hand. The label on the bottle read: Eau Naturelle.

"Ten points to me," Tony repeated.

The game—although Addison suspected that 'game' was too generous a term for this diversion—was a simple tally. If someone walked through reception carrying a bottle of mineral water, ten points were awarded. If the bottle of mineral water was clear, Addison received the ten points. If the bottle was green the ten points went to Tony. The points were tallied at the end of the day. The winner, Addison surmised, would either be the person with the most points or the one who hadn't died from boredom during the preceding hours.

This was a green bottle. The ten points went to Tony.

If there was one marginally interesting detail to be gleaned from the diversion, Addison thought it was the revelation that so many of the station's staff, particularly the female staff, walked around carrying bottles of mineral water.

If not for Tony's game, it was a detail she knew she would not have noticed.

She had asked him if there was a reason and he had shrugged.

"Eau Naturelle are the station's chief sponsors," Tony told her. "So that could be a factor. Plus, I guess it helps with on-air nerves. I tried sitting in a studio once and I got the worst case of dry-mouth I've ever had. I could barely speak. A bottle of water would probably have helped there. I found it really hard to swallow." He had grinned slyly then and asked, "Do you ever find it hard to swallow?"

At the time, Addison had merely shaken her head and ignored him. She tried doing the same thing now as he revelled in his ten point accomplishment.

"Ten points," Tony cried. "Add those to my scorecard. I'm on a roll."

"What the fuck did you say?"

Addison glanced up.

The tall, elegant brunette had rounded on Tony. Her phone was away from her ear now, her important conversation discarded. She was pointing at him with one crimson-polished nail.

Not crimson, Addison noted. The fingernail was the same cranberry colour as her chinos. The woman was nothing if not coordinated. Her snarl was the same brilliant white as the manic gleam behind her ice-blue eyes.

"Are you playing your dipshit little games again?"

"Zoe." Tony's smile was a pained grimace. "I was just … I mean we were just …" Tony glanced nervously in Addison's direction, clearly hoping she would back him up. "… we were just counting bottles of water and—"

"You get paid for doing fuck all, don't you?"

Addison blushed on Tony's behalf.

She struggled not to watch the scene but it had the

forbidden allure of a gory horror movie or a gruesome traffic accident. As much as she didn't want to see what was going on, a voyeuristic part of her needed to ghoulishly drink in every detail.

Zoe was clearly about to tear Tony a new one. From the corner of her eye Addison could see him squirming beneath the presenter's ire.

"Let me give you a word of fucking advice," Zoe growled. "You sit here all day, playing silly little games that relate to things that have nothing to do with you—"

"We were only counting water bottles."

Tony tried to speak over her and stop the tirade but Zoe seemed unstoppable. She punctuated every point by jabbing her fingernail down at him. Her words were spat with such ferocity that beads of spittle escaped her mouth as she spoke.

"—and you think that gives you the right to judge people."

"We weren't judging people," Addison broke in.

She didn't want to get involved in the argument but she could see Tony needed some help. Even though she felt no special affinity with Tony, Addison didn't like the idea of anyone suffering such a torrent of abuse for no good reason.

"We weren't judging people," Addison repeated. "We were just playing a dumb counting game."

Zoe rounded on her.

She took a glance at the name badge on Addison's breast and sneered.

"You're Addison, are you?"

"Yes."

Zoe nodded. "I thought as much. I was going to listen to your radio show earlier. Then I remembered—you don't have a radio show. I do."

Addison blinked. That response was both harsh and unexpected. The vitriol pouring from the woman was virtually radioactive. She didn't know whether to be appalled or impressed. In the moment she was too stunned to respond.

Zoe pointed at Tony. "You'll stop using me as part of your stupid fucking games."

He nodded.

She turned back to Addison. "And if you ever see me berating a worthless piece of scum again, you'll keep your mouth shut, do you understand?"

Addison's hands had curled into fists.

Tony stepped over to her and placed a reassuring hand on Addison's shoulder. Smiling nervously at Zoe he said, "Addison understands. She won't talk to you again unless you've spoken to her. She understands."

Addison didn't understand. But she supposed, if there was a choice between keeping this job or pretending she understood, she knew which option would help to pay that month's bills.

"I want to hear it from her," Zoe insisted.

"I understand," Addison said quickly. She didn't allow herself to think about the words. If she'd given herself a moment to consider what she was saying, Addison knew she would have said, "I understand you're a bitch with some sort of psychotic esteem issues."

Zoe flexed her scowl for a final time and then stepped away from the reception desk. She continued walking through the lobby, still glowering at Tony and Addison. When she finally disappeared through the door marked 'studios', taking her scowl and her green bottle of mineral water, Tony released a pent up sigh of relief.

"What the hell is her problem?" Addison asked.

"Zoe's a bit of a ball-breaker," Tony admitted. "But that was probably my fault. I shouldn't have been playing the water bottle game. I know it upsets her. She's indicated that before."

Addison frowned trying to think how the game could have caused any upset.

Zoe had said they were judging her. Addison wasn't sure how the concept of judgement could be involved. Was there some superiority that she didn't know about between Evian, Perrier, Eau Naturelle or one of the other popular brands of mineral water? She felt stupid for even entertaining such an idea but it was the closest she could come to a logical explanation.

A call came in on the desk.

Tony had answered it before Addison remembered she was there as a receptionist. She smiled an apology to him as he glanced in her direction and spoke on the phone.

Mineral water was clearly important to so many of the radio station's presenters, she thought. Perhaps it had something to do with the corporate sponsorship from Eau Naturelle? Few of the presenters turned up at the studio without a bottle of that brand in hand.

Addison had also assumed the drink was needed to help them speak more fluently in the nerve-wracking, throat-drying presence of a live studio microphone. She imagined the job would be frightening and exhilarating at the same time. But Zoe's comments suggested the mineral water was for something else: that it was more than a mere drink.

"Stern wants to see you," Tony said.

Addison cleared her head of her quiet musings and glanced at him.

Tony nodded toward the handset he had just replaced in the receiver. He spoke slowly, as though long words might cause possible confusion. "Stern, the station manager, he just called and said he wanted a word with you."

Addison sighed. She stared unhappily up at Stern's office on the first floor.

The windowed wall of his office overlooked the reception area through one-way glass. She stared up at the mirrored surface and wondered if Stern was behind the glass staring down at her. She wondered if he had seen her confrontation with Zoe and now wanted to tell her that her services were no longer needed on the reception desk.

It would not, she reasoned pragmatically, be the first job from which she had been fired. Reflecting on her inability to learn life lessons, she supposed it would not be the last. Resignedly, Addison pulled herself from her seat and started toward the stairs.

"Here," Tony said, stopping her before she left the desk. "Stern said you'd need this."

She frowned as she looked at the bottle of mineral water he had pushed into her hand. It was a clear bottle and, of course, bore the Eau Naturelle label. Before she could ask any questions the reception desk telephone was ringing again. Tony was quickly immersed in smiling his way through another plastically-pleasant conversation and Addison realised she had to visit Stern as she'd been commanded.

Her journey up to his office took her past the accounts department.

She saw the head of Human Resources standing and chatting with one of the clerks from that department. The two women were both smartly dressed wearing short-length skirts and tight, figure-hugging tops. As they spoke, the head of human resources drank from a green bottle of mineral water. She placed the rim of the bottle against her lower lip and tilted the base upwards so that the liquid poured freely into her mouth.

She swallowed in slow, leisurely gulps.

Her throat moved with languid mellow ripples.

Watching her, Addison knew this was how the woman's throat would move after she'd drunk red wine on a romantic date. It was how her throat would move if she'd licked the sweat from a lover's naked body. It was how her throat would move if she was on her knees, sweat-lathered with passion and swallowing her lover's cum.

Even though she was only engaged in a dull conversation with a clerk from accounts, her eyes were closed in a state of near-orgasmic bliss. Her chest had broadened and Addison was sure she could see the shape of the woman's nipples jutting against the fabric of her bra and top.

Blushing, Addison looked away.

There's something in the water, she thought.

She didn't really believe there was anything in the water when the thought first crossed her mind. The phrase was one of those catchall excuses she had grown up with. It was a response that was used to explain everything from the high incidence of redheads in one region through to acts of political stupidity in localised voting patterns.

Now, in this case, she wondered if there might be a

grain of truth in the words.

Warily, she considered the weight of the bottle in her hand.

She'd yet to take a drink from this one and already it had transformed her into a licentious pervert. She had been ogling the head of Human Resources and picturing the woman licking the sweat from a lover's body and then kneeling down to swallow his cum. Addison wondered how severely the mineral water would affect her libido if she dared to take a sip.

She wasn't sure she wanted to experiment and find out.

She wasn't sure she dared to make that investigation.

There was a small reception area outside Stern's office. Two people waited there beneath the watchful eye of Stern's dour-faced personal receptionist.

Addison recognised William Daye as one of the station's more successful presenters. He was tall and darkly attractive in a bland-James-Bond fashion. The woman sitting away from Daye, huddled alone in a corner of Stern's reception, was Lydia Knight.

When she first saw the woman that morning, Addison had thought Knight looked overly glamorous for a woman who was in a recording studio presenting an unseen radio show. It surprised her that Lydia wasn't sitting closer to Daye as she had assumed the two presenters were friends as well as co-hosts on the afternoon show, Daye and

Knight.

Lydia, it seemed, was sitting away from Daye because she was preoccupied.

She sat in a corner of the room. Her gaze was lowered and her ankles were crossed. She had the base of a pale green bottle of mineral water pressed between the tops of her thighs. Unconsciously, and seeming unmindful of anyone else seeing what she was doing, Lydia rocked the bottle back and forth against her crotch.

Addison held her breath. She wanted to watch the woman more closely. She wanted to see what was going on. She had never before encountered anything so—

"May I help you?"

Addison glanced up to see that Stern's dour-faced receptionist was addressing her. The woman's words cut through whatever thoughts she had been forming about the peculiarity of Lydia's actions.

"Addison," she explained. "I'm here to see Mr. Stern."

"From main reception?"

She nodded.

"Go and sit in that corner and drink your water."

Addison frowned and tried to think how she was supposed to respond to such an unprecedented command. She started to say something, then realised the words would likely land her in more trouble than she currently needed.

"I'm here to see Mr. Stern," she repeated, wondering if there had been some confusion. "He just called down and—"

"Go and sit in that corner and drink your water," the receptionist repeated, pointing. "I shall inform Mr. Stern that you're waiting. He will see you when he has time to see you."

The woman scowled at Addison and then turned her gaze away. Addison could see an earpiece trailing from the receptionist's ear and when the receptionist began speaking again, Addison knew she was no longer part of the conversation.

Daye flashed her a sympathetic smile.

His shrug said that he didn't quite understand the receptionist's rudeness. And the shifting of his gaze, and his exaggerated pretence at suddenly seeing something interesting in his magazine, said he had no intention of discussing the matter.

Knight seemed oblivious to everything around her as Addison took a chair in a facing corner. It was impossible not to watch as Knight rolled the base of her water bottle against her crotch. The woman's eyes were closed with lurid concentration but her jaw hung half-open. She occasionally released soft, moaning sounds that were obscenely reminiscent of orgasm.

Addison didn't know whether to be intrigued or repulsed.

The sound of Stern's office door opening snatched her attention away. She looked up in time to see the receptionist tell William Daye, "Mr. Stern will see you now."

As the receptionist spoke to Daye, Zoe flounced out of Stern's office.

Zoe stormed over to where Addison sat and pointed a finger down at her. Her cheeks were flushed with twin spots of matching colour. Her nipples stood hard against the smooth fabric of the blouse beneath her little black Chanel jacket. There was a spreading damp stain on the crotch of her cranberry chinos.

Addison tried not to gape.

"Let me give you a word of fucking advice," Zoe growled.

Addison flinched, expecting a tirade similar to the one Zoe had inflicted on Tony. Instead of an outpouring of bile and fury, the woman simply puckered her lips into a scowl and said, "Don't think you've heard the last of this."

Then she was gone.

Addison was left alone in Stern's reception with Stern's receptionist, Lydia Knight, and her own bottle of mineral water.

"Jesus," Addison muttered. "Is that scary bitch incontinent? Or does she just cream herself from stamping on everyone below her?"

"She's not incontinent," Lydia muttered. "She's just humiliated."

Addison glanced at Lydia.

The woman hadn't opened her eyes. She still sat with her legs slightly apart, the bottle of mineral water pressed firmly against her crotch, her chest rising and falling with symptoms that looked as though she was in the throes of a near-orgasmic release.

"She's just humiliated," Lydia repeated.

"Excuse me?"

"Drink your water," Lydia said. "Stern will have expected you to have done that much when you're summoned."

"What's going on here?" Addison asked. "What am I missing?"

"You're not missing anything."

Lydia's bottle continued to rock back and forth. The motion was slow, deliberate and consistent with its rhythm. She continued until her entire body stiffened. The shock of stiffness was followed by a small, trembling shiver. Then she took a long, drawling breath that sounded lewdly similar to an orgasmic sigh. Finally, Lydia opened her eyes. She studied Addison with a solemn appraisal that was almost too intense.

Addison allowed the woman to look, still trying to work out whether this was uncommonly bizarre behaviour, or if it fitted with everything else she had so far experienced at the radio station.

"Drink your water," Lydia urged. She closed her eyes. "That'll be for the best."

"You two aren't talking, are you?" called the receptionist.

Lydia said nothing. She continued to rock back and forth.

Addison decided it would be best if she didn't respond. She didn't think she would be able to say anything constructive as a reply to such a school-mistress-type question. Unless she watched every syllable she muttered for the rest of the afternoon, Addison knew she was in serious danger of saying something irrevocable and career-killing on her first day with the radio station.

"I'm sure you both know that Mr. Stern doesn't allow talking whilst you're waiting," the receptionist called.

Addison had known no such thing.

The rule sounded positively draconian. She settled back in her chair and wondered if she should simply give up on the idea of becoming a radio presenter. Admittedly, the goal of becoming a radio presenter was a long-cherished ambition. But it seemed that the goal of being a radio presenter at this station came at the cost of dignity and respect.

"Yes," Lydia sighed.

The word roused Addison from her musings. She turned and glanced at the woman. Lydia had the base of the bottle of mineral pressed so hard against her sex it looked like beads of pressured-perspiration were sliding down the sides of the plastic. Her eyes were closed but the lids fluttered as though she was in the throes of euphoria.

"Yes," Lydia repeated.

Addison tore her gaze away.

Was Lydia really getting herself off? Was that acceptable public behaviour anywhere? Had no one else in the radio station noticed? And why was Lydia's arousal so frighteningly contagious? Addison could taste the electric excitement in the air. Her entire body throbbed as though she was yearning to share some of the woman's infectious sexual enthusiasm.

"Are you …?"

Her voice trailed off. She couldn't think how to broach the subject without sounding voyeuristic, challenging or judgemental. Lydia hadn't bothered to open her eyes and Addison was happy to convince herself that the woman hadn't heard her question.

"Never mind," she said quietly.

"Drink your water," Lydia whispered. "And let me finish what I have to do."

Addison wouldn't let herself brood on the questions that rushed through her thoughts. She herself was sitting in a corner of Stern's reception area, with her legs parted further than usual for this skirt, and she had noticed that she was resting her own bottle of water against her groin. Her temperature seemed slightly raised. She was acutely conscious of the weight of the bottle against the delta between her legs. And, if she was wholly honest with herself, the idea of rubbing out a quick happy from that same place was not unappealing.

She shook her head and stopped herself from pursuing that thought.

Even if she was very quick—

"No," she told herself.

Even if she was very discreet—

She shook her head. It was insane to be thinking of such an act. The prospect of actually doing such a thing was beyond insanity. Nervously, she snapped the cap on her bottle of water and took a swig. Her hand was shaking as she put the bottle to her lips.

The liquid more than quenched her thirst.

She allowed it to moisten her lips. She revelled in the refreshing absence of taste. She didn't even mind when a couple of droplets splashed from her mouth and landed on her décolletage through the open throat of her blouse. The chill of the droplets was surprisingly pleasant in the stuffy atmosphere of the radio station.

"Yes," moaned Lydia.

Her voice was lowered and there was an

unmistakable lustre of satisfaction underscoring the exclamation. Addison was trying not to look but she couldn't resist glancing at the woman.

Lydia wore a broad, surprised grin. Her body trembled. After a moment's silence, Lydia eased the base of the bottle away from her groin and took a long, leisurely swig. She finally opened her eyes and winked at Addison.

"There are perks to working here," Lydia said. She stood up on faltering legs, smiling self-consciously at her own lack of balance. "Stick around," Lydia told Addison. "You might enjoy it here."

She dropped her empty bottle of water into a waste bin.

"Tell Stern that I did as he asked," she told the receptionist. "I'll expect the change of our show's name to be made public next week: Knight and Daye."

The receptionist nodded and made a note.

Before Addison had a chance to work out what the words might mean, she realised that Knight had left the small waiting area and Daye was walking out of Stern's office.

As usual he looked swarthy and debonair but his swagger seemed to falter a little, as though he had heard Lydia's parting words. There was no time to consider what she was seeing because the receptionist was pointing at her.

"Mr. Stern will see you now."

Addison leapt from her seat, drained her drink and tossed the empty bottle into a bin. Before she could get into the office the receptionist was handing her a replacement bottle of mineral water. Unable to refuse, Addison took it and stepped into the room.

The door to Stern's office closed behind her.

The room was large, airy and spacious.

A long windowed wall overlooked the reception desk where she had been working. With Stern's office and the reception area equally bright, it had been impossible to see into Stern's office from the lobby. But, Tony had insisted, Stern was able to see everything from his vantage point.

Addison could now see that Tony was right.

The view from Stern's office was a commanding one that gave him a glimpse of every corner of the lobby. It made her think of the way she had always imagined a god staring down on his worshippers. She wondered if that was how Stern felt when he stood and secretly spied on his subordinates.

"Take a seat."

Obligingly, she took the seat in the chair facing his desk.

He stood up and, not for the first time, Addison was surprised by his height. He was tall and broad and obscenely young for someone in such a responsible position. Dressed in a tailored Armani suit, charcoal grey with a white shirt and cerulean tie, Addison thought his masculine figure would look better on a bodybuilder's beach, curling weights and pumping iron.

When he sat on the edge of his desk, close enough for her to think he was invading her personal space, Addison was disturbed to think he smelled as good as he looked. She caught essences of citrus fruits and something sweetly honeyed. She didn't think it was right for an employee to think her boss smelled good.

"Sip your drink, please." He gestured to the bottle in her hand. He licked his lips and said, "I'd like it very much if you could sip your drink whilst we talk. I'm a firm believer in the importance of hydration."

It was an unusual request, Addison thought. She tried not to let herself think that the command made him sound like some sort of serial killer, pervert or psycho. She couldn't argue that the instruction made him sound weird. But she told herself it was nothing more than a quirk supported by the man's belief in hydration. And, considering that all the Eau Naturelle adverts around the studio reiterated the benefits of hydration, she supposed it was understandable why he thought it was so important.

Anxious to keep him happy, she twisted the cap from her bottle and sipped.

The fluid was cool on her lips.

She swallowed quickly, never letting her eyes drop from his.

She was keenly conscious of her throat undulating beneath his gaze. She wondered if he had noticed the way the muscles rose and fell. She wondered if he was thinking of those other occasions when she would be likely to swallow so easily.

Her cheeks turned crimson.

He smiled. "You have aspirations to become a radio presenter, don't you?"

Addison nodded. She had told him as much when she applied for the position as the receptionist. She didn't believe he had specifically remembered her ambitions. Either he had just re-read her file or, more likely, everyone working at the radio station had a desire to be a presenter.

"That is a fairly common ambition around here," Stern said, as though reading her thoughts. "Some people will do anything to get their own show." He paused and considered her solemnly. "Some people will do *anything*."

Addison frowned.

Was he expecting her to fuck him in exchange for a radio show?

She had no problems with that concept. It seemed like a ridiculously easy bargain to strike. Stern was attractive and she was horny. It was like paying for a sandwich by being hungry. If she had known about this sort of arrangement earlier, Addison thought she could have saved herself the boredom of sitting at the reception desk and pretending to smile for the idiots making their way into the building.

"I'd do *anything* to have my own radio show," she admitted. She gave the word the lurid stress she believed it deserved. She licked her lips and hoped he understood what she meant. "And I do mean I would do anything."

Stern shook his head.

His smile was apologetic.

"I don't think you quite understand," he began patiently. "You say you'd do anything. But you think that involves … I don't know … having my finger up your ass, or letting me fuck your mouth."

Addison gasped, shocked by his forthright choice of words.

She glanced nervously around, wondering if someone had entered the room and Stern was showing off to impress the newcomer. It was disconcerting to see that they remained alone.

"Don't get me wrong," Stern said. "I'm sure I'd enjoy both of those activities. And probably more. I don't doubt your ass and your mouth are equally fuckable. But, for me, I'd want more than those trivial diversions."

"More?"

Addison was doubtful. Her ass and her mouth were trivial diversions? What did that mean? And, he had mentioned her ass and her mouth: was he negotiating for access to—

"You want my pussy?"

He laughed softly. "If you really want a role as one of my presenters you'll freely give me access to any orifice of your body. That's a given."

She swallowed. His honesty was both disturbing and exciting. She had taken on the role of a receptionist, more than willing to exchange sexual services if it could further her career. But she hadn't expected Stern to know that she was willing to exchange sexual services for such advancement. And, even if he did know, she had never expected him to show such poor social skills as to state the arrangement so baldly.

"Yes, Mr. Stern," she stammered.

"I want more than your pussy," he admitted. "I want more than your pussy, your ass or your mouth."

A tit-fuck? Addison thought, puzzled. Was that what he wanted? If it was only a tit-fuck it seemed like such a negligible price to pay. Or did he just want a hand-job? That was even less of a commitment. She could do that whilst updating her status on her mobile. She almost asked if he meant a hand-job or a tit-fuck.

Stern spoke first.

"I want your humiliation."

"You want my what?"

He moved before she realised what was happening. He stood up and snatched the uncapped water bottle she'd been holding. Before Addison could react, he had splashed the contents over her crotch.

Later, she would admire his accuracy.

In that moment she was simply shocked.

"Jesus," she cried. "What the actual—"

As she started to climb out of the chair, desperate to escape the spreading puddle of water in her lap, he knelt down by her side. One hand was on her arm. The strength he used wasn't enormous. She knew she could pull away from him if she wanted to flee his office. But there was something deliciously liberating in simply staying beneath his hand whilst he whispered into her ear.

"I want to bask in your humiliation," he explained. "I want to indulge in your discomfort. I want to thrill in your experience of sexual embarrassment."

She could feel her heartbeat quickening.

Stern had seemed desirable before. Now he was acting as though he could be dangerous. It was a trait that made him infinitely more appealing. She struggled not to melt into the chair.

"Humiliation?" she asked doubtfully.

"Your crotch is piss-wet from front to back."

When he said the words, Addison realised for the first time how accurate his aim had been. He had hurled the water at her lap and the fluid had struck precisely over her pussy. She was sitting on the leather seat in his office, obscenely conscious of the chilly pool of wetness that flooded her inner thighs.

Her seat was soaked.

Her cotton panties were fat and swollen with excess liquid.

She was acutely aware of every saturated sensation that touched her sex. With Stern holding her arm and staring into her eyes it was almost as though the man was idly teasing the lips of her labia by thought alone. That concept was enough to make her clitoris pulse against the wet threads of her sodden underwear.

"Your crotch is piss-wet from front to back," he said again. "And, when you walk out of this office, you'll be painfully aware that everyone is staring at your crotch. You'll be painfully aware that everyone is thinking that you either wet yourself, or you got so excited you squirted."

Addison blushed.

She wanted to tell him that he was talking bullshit. She wanted to say that no one would ever think such things when it would be obvious that the station manager had simply poured a bottle of mineral over her lap because he was a pervert that got off on such weird abuse.

But she knew no one would give credence to her version of events.

She remembered what she had thought when she saw Zoe's soaked crotch. She had wondered if the scary bitch was incontinent, or merely creaming herself.

Miserably, Addison realised that the only difference between her humiliation and the one that Zoe had suffered was the fact that Zoe had a reputation for being a scary bitch. Addison didn't even have that reputation to help her stave the wagging tongues that would begin gossiping about what might have happened.

Angry, she tried to pull away.

Stern held her firm.

"This is one of the key humiliations I expect from my radio presenters," he said. "And, if you can spend the rest of the day doing your job on reception with that wet spot on your skirt, I'll let you share a studio with Zoe tonight."

She stared at him and tried to feign incredulity. "Do you really think I'd be interested in such a repulsive proposition?"

He laughed. "You're trying to bluff me. I like that."

"I'm not trying to bluff any—"

She didn't get to finish.

Stern put a finger on her lips and shook his head.

"Don't say another word. Just go back to your desk and endure your embarrassment for the rest of the day. If you still want to be a radio presenter when it's six o'clock, you can come in here, suck my cock, and I'll let you share the studio with Zoe."

The air in the room had turned to electricity.

She was having difficulty breathing as the increased excitement made her acutely aware of the arousal that Stern generated. She glowered at him through heavily lidded eyes, wishing she didn't find him so attractive and loathing the fact that he was able to make her yearn for the unpleasantness he was offering.

"If you're not bluffing," Stern continued, "I'll let you leave here now. You can go home and start the tribunal complaint for sexual harassment."

She regarded him sceptically.

He shrugged. "I'll contest your claim by pretending that you spilt the water in your lap. I'll be able to provide testimony evidence from two witnesses who saw the accident happen. They'll also explain that your reaction was surprisingly volatile."

"You unconscionable bastard."

He nodded. "I'm an unconscionable bastard who'll see you here just after six tonight." Then he was pushing a clear bottle of water into her hand and escorting her out of the office.

The receptionist glanced up as Addison walked out.

She immediately saw the large damp stain that darkened Addison's skirt, and she rolled her eyes and shook her head.

Addison could feel her cheeks colouring hot pink. She opened her mouth to explain that it wasn't what it looked like. Then she remembered what lay in the balance if she did say those words.

She lowered her gaze, tried to cover the stain with her hands, and hurried out of the room. Rushing down the stairs she was conscious of the weight of her panties. The gusset was sodden. The fabric pulled at her. Every movement made her aware that her sex was wet. Every moment of awareness reminded her that she was scheduled to return to Stern's office at six o'clock and suck his cock.

Her stomach cramped with an unexpected pang of excitement.

When she arrived back in the lobby she glanced back up at the opaque window on Stern's office. She wondered if he was behind the glass now, smirking down at her and enjoying her discomfort. Or perhaps he had someone else in his office and he was forcing them to endure a repeat of the humiliation he had visited upon her.

She didn't know which option was more exciting.

The inner muscles of her sex clutched and clenched as though she was already in the clasp of an orgasm. Shaking, she reached the front desk and hurried to get back to her seat before Tony had a chance to notice that she—

"Oh my fucking god!" Tony gasped. "You've pi—"

"Don't say another word," she warned.

She squelched into her seat behind the reception desk and folded her legs. The movement made her conscious of her wet pussy. At the same time she was conscious of Tony studying her with a series of awkward, sideways glances.

"Are you ok?"

Her cheeks had been pink before. Now they were the colour of tomatoes.

"Never better."

"You ... I mean ..." He was pointing at her. One wagging finger kept dipping toward the direction of her lap. "You ..."

"Never better," she insisted.

When the phone rang she answered it so swiftly the caller was surprised to find her there. Every phone call that came through to the desk was another sublime excuse that saved her from the embarrassment of having to talk with Tony and avoid discussing what had happened in Stern's office. She cheerfully greeted the remainder of the afternoon's visitors with a disarming smile and a focus of attention that didn't allow them to shift their gaze from her eyes. She did everything within her power to stop herself from thinking about the syrupy cooling wetness that lingered between her legs. She wouldn't dwell on the idea that, if she spent a dedicated minute in the station's lavatories, she could wring out the happy that her body desperately needed.

Her cheeks darkened at the idea. She told herself that she wasn't tempted.

"Ten points to you," Tony said eventually.

She scowled at him.

He was pointing at the clear water bottle that had been given to her by Stern's receptionist. "You've decided it's the best way to win this game, haven't you? You're bringing your own points to the game."

She could hear the forced cheer in his voice.

"Yes," she agreed. "Ten points to me."

"Did you know there's some wetness on your skirt?"

She clenched her teeth. "Yes, Tony. I know there's some wetness there."

"Did it happen in Stern's office?"

Not trusting herself to voice the words, Addison nodded.

"That happens to me, sometimes," Tony admitted. His cheeks turned crimson as he studied the floor, and Addison knew he wasn't joking. "Stern frightens a lot of people in that way."

She stood up and left the reception desk.

Ignoring Tony's calls of protest, not wanting to listen to him for another moment, she headed out of the main doors toward the station's smoking area. Addison no longer smoked, but she suddenly relished the opportunity to stand with the outcasts of the smoking community and embrace their role as pariahs. She was feeling like a pariah herself.

One of the smokers glanced at the wet patch in the centre of her skirt and silently handed her a cigarette.

Addison accepted the smoke with a mumbled thank you.

Was this what she really wanted? The humiliation part was fun, she supposed. But the idea of working under the regime of a dictatorial boss was not something she had ever envied. Admittedly, she had been prepared to fuck Stern if it meant he would give her a position as a radio presenter. But she wasn't happy that he was blatantly using that knowledge to satisfy his own sick and sadistic appetites. It took the edge off her using that bargaining chip to help further her career.

"I had no idea you were a smoker," Lydia Knight said.

Addison tried to suck on the cigarette as though she still remembered how to do it. "Yes," she said, struggling not to cough out the acrid taste. "I'm a smoker. We're a dying breed."

Lydia shook her head and sighed. "May I offer you a word of advice?"

"I guess."

"You want to be on the radio, don't you?"

"I guess."

Lydia slapped her across the face. The blow stung. It was so harsh and unexpected Addison dropped the cigarette from her fingers.

"You either want it or you don't," Lydia snapped. "Which is it?"

"I want it," said Addison, rubbing her jaw. "I want it."

"Then act like you want it," Lydia growled. "You feel humiliated? Good. Embrace the feeling. Learn to live with it. Maybe it's not the most pleasant feeling in the world but I'd bet, if you're anything like the other bitches in this place, your panties are wetter now than when Stern squirted water on them."

Addison blushed.

She was aware that the others who loitered about the smoking area could hear what Lydia was saying. She was also liberated by the idea that it didn't matter who overheard. She was suffering a humiliation that most of them had endured. The knowledge was somehow empowering.

"You think I should just let him humiliate me?"

"No. I've just told you what I think. I think you should take everything you can from Stern. Take the chance to do the radio show. Take the pleasure of the humiliation. Take every piece of satisfaction that's being offered to you."

"Is that what you do?"

Lydia raised her bottle of mineral water in a mock

salute and grinned. "That's what I do every day."

Addison returned to the reception desk with her shoulders back. She leant close to Tony and whispered in his ear.

"I've got to go to the bathroom and take off my wet underwear. They've been soaked through all afternoon. You don't mind covering for five minutes whilst I'm gone, do you?"

She wasn't watching his face for a response.

Instead, she watched his lap as the shape of an erection sprang forward against the front of his pants. His jaw sagged and his eyes studied her with the haunted expression of a man pained by agonised longing.

She hurried through to the bathroom and found an empty cubicle. Peeling the soaked panties away from her sex, savouring the delicious rush of cool air that touched her, Addison stood up with her shoulders against the closed door and placed one foot on the rim of the toilet seat.

Slowly, but with painstaking deliberation, she began to touch herself.

She stroked fingers up her thigh and reached beneath the hem of her short skirt. Her heartbeat raced as she realised she was already close to the brink of a heady, powerful orgasm.

As soon as her fingers touched the bare flesh of her sticky sex, her legs nearly buckled and she sagged against the door. When she stroked the tip of one nail against the throbbing pulse of her clitoris, the sensation was almost too much to bear. Addison thrust a hand into her mouth to quell the scream of euphoria that needed to tear from her lungs.

She stiffened her back against the toilet door. She tensed every muscle in her body as though fighting the impending orgasm.

Obviously, she wanted the satisfaction. If she was being honest, she craved the release of that satisfaction. But, a part of her felt as though it was indecorous and unseemly to be coaxing herself to orgasm in the staff toilets.

Her slick finger slid deep into her wetness.

The position meant straining her wrist at an awkward angle but Addison was happy to do that much. The awkward angle meant the ball of her thumb was pressed against the throbbing bead of her clitoris. She didn't know whether it was that additional pressure, the excitement of the moment, or some other stimulus.

But she did know that caress was all it took.

As the orgasm seared through her frame, Addison remembered Lydia's words. She should be taking advantage of everything Stern had to offer: whether it was a chance to work on a radio show, the unexpected humiliation of walking around with a drenched crotch, or even the opportunity to rub out a personal happy moment in the staff lavatories.

She clenched her throat tight to stop her cries of ecstasy from escaping the bathroom cubicle. Her body contorted in paroxysms of pure and unadulterated pleasure. She squeezed harder against the nub of her pulsing clitoris. The thrill of a second orgasm washed across the pleasure of the first.

Addison snatched her hand away from herself and allowed the hem of her skirt to fall back, covering her modesty. The pleasure had been intense and powerful and, honestly, she could feel the needy wave of another orgasm rising quickly. But she didn't dare tease out any more satisfaction, for fear of leaving herself too drained to continue with the day.

Instead, taking her sodden panties from the floor, she walked back to the reception desk and stood beside Tony. She wondered if he would detect the scent of her arousal. She didn't doubt the trickles of wetness that now trailed down her inner thighs heralded her excitement. When he nervously looked up at her she noticed his pants still bulged from the weight of his erection.

"I took my panties off," she whispered.

She had the sodden cotton in her hand. She pushed the wadded fabric under his nose as she tossed the skimpy cloth into the wastebasket by his side. And she knew he would spend the remainder of the day waiting for an opportunity to surreptitiously retrieve them from there.

It would prove to be a long afternoon for Tony, she

thought.

But she also knew the diversion of watching him would be more entertaining than his mindless bottle-counting games. She suspected it would be almost as entertaining as the humiliation she was learning to savour.

It was clear to Addison that Tony was desperate to find the right moment to liberate her drying intimates from the waste bin. She guessed that a further part of him was desperate to find an excuse to get down on his knees and inadvertently peak up her skirt. As the day drew on, with no signs of his erection abating, and with his constant furtive glances never failing to make her smirk, Addison decided he had earned a reward.

She dropped a pen on the floor between them.

Tony studied it for a moment. His expression made her think of a hungry dog contemplating a bone. She was surprised that he didn't start to drool with a Pavlovian response.

Addison remained sitting in her chair as she studied him expectantly.

Eventually, when he made no move to pick it up, she turned in her seat so she was facing him and spread her legs slightly apart.

His concealed erection hadn't faltered throughout the day. A part of her pitied him for the torment he had clearly been suffering. And a part of her envied him the rich humiliation he was clearly enjoying at her expense.

"Pick it up," she told him.

There was no need for a please or a thank you. If Stern chose to speak to her in that way, Addison knew she would have been close to orgasm from the thrill. Dominating Tony in the fashion she hoped Stern would dominate her, Addison realised she was doing as Lydia had suggested by taking every scrap of pleasure there was to be had at the station.

"Excuse me?"

"Get down on your knees, between my legs, and pick up the pen I dropped."

To illustrate the subtext of her words, Addison traced a finger against her thigh and teased the hem of her skirt higher. She watched as Tony's eyebrows inched upwards. She wondered how much of her he would be able to see from his vantage point in the chair beside her.

However much it was, it obviously wasn't enough for him.

He fell to the floor and scrabbled blindly to pick up the pen.

His gaze never shifted from the apex of her legs. His eyes were wide. He licked his lips. She was momentarily stung by the satisfying sweet thrill of exploiting his unreciprocated desire.

When he passed her the pen, Addison pushed down the hem of her skirt.

She stood up and said, "I've got to go and see Stern now. Goodnight, Tony."

She didn't bother listening for his reply. She was sure that all she could hear was a frustrated sob that was too soft to be heard over the clatter of her heels on the stairs up to Stern's office.

The receptionist handed her a bottle of clear mineral water before opening the office door for her. Addison took it and then paused. "There's no light on in here."

"I'm saving on my electricity bills," Stern called from within the darkness of his office. "Now get in here and close the door."

She did as she was told.

She could feel the swelling sense of arousal that now flooded through her. The air in the office was almost too thick to drink into her lungs.

"You came back," Stern observed.

"You told me to come back at six if I wanted to do the radio show with Zoe."

"I'd wanted to enjoy more of your humiliation today." She could see his silhouette in the darkness. "I've been watching you down on the reception desk. I'd hoped the embarrassment of having wet your panties would have proved more uncomfortable for you. You seemed to tolerate it too well."

She shrugged. "Perhaps I need a different form of humiliation," she challenged.

"This is what I thought," Stern agreed. "Get down on your knees and crawl over to the window."

She did as he commanded. When she got there she could see that his erection was exposed. The hardness was everything she had hoped it would be. She didn't bother waiting for his instruction to suck. Her lips were already around him and she was moving her mouth up and down his length, lapping at him with her tongue and relishing the silky salted taste of his pre-cum as it slipped from his shaft.

"I figured you'd need to be humiliated in different ways." Stern spoke as though he wasn't distracted by the pleasure of the oral attention she gave him. His hardness remained a constant in her mouth. She could feel the sullen pulse of him as he swelled and fattened against her tongue.

"The wet crotch works as a humiliation on some staff, but not all."

She nodded. Despite the even tone of his voice, the anxious strain of his member told Addison that she had nearly sucked the climax from him; and she didn't want to stop until his warm seed was at the back of her throat.

"But I thought you needed a different kind of public shaming," Stern told her. "That's why I wanted you to suck my cock here in front of the window." As he spoke, he flicked a light switch.

In that moment, as the light flooded over her, Addison understood.

Her actions could now be seen clearly from the lobby.

During the day, when daylight flooded the lobby, the windowed wall of his office looked like one way glass. But during the evening, when the lights in the lobby were dimmed and the lights in Stern's office burned bright, the windowed wall was as opaque as a goldfish bowl.

With her mouth still wrapped around his length, Addison glanced down into the lobby.

Tony was staring up at her from the reception desk. Beside him Lydia was raising a glass of mineral water in a good-natured salute. The embarrassment of being caught in such an act was so severe that Addison could feel the rush of an orgasm yearning to accelerate through her body.

Stern took the bottle of mineral water from Addison's fingers.

She had forgotten she was still holding the thing.

He slowly unscrewed the cap without moving his shaft from her mouth. He bent over her, and the motion served to push his length even more deeply into her, forcing her to take more of him into her mouth. He extended a long and sinewy arm to nimbly take the hem of her skirt between two fingers.

"Arch your back. Lift your backside," he stated simply.

She complied.

Smoothly, he slid the hem of her skirt up over the swell of her ass so that her bare backside and more were displayed to the room ... and the window. He tipped the bottle and cool water cascaded onto her overheated flesh. The shock of it made her gasp and twitch as water spilled over the hills of her ass, ran down the crevice between her cheeks, and soaked her rumpled skirt in the small of her back. Stern kept pouring and, as cold water drenched the heat of her sex and eddied away between her thighs, Addison exploded.

She sucked more vigorously, and realised she was swallowing the taste of his importunate cum. More importantly, she was basking in the thrill of her own, water-fuelled orgasm. She doubted her humiliation could have been more exciting or more severe.

"I'll need to begin prepping for my show quite soon, Mr. Stern."

Addison recognised Zoe's voice. She hadn't noticed the woman sitting at the side of Stern's office until she spoke. Now, with mineral water dripping from the lips of her sex, and Stern's cum still coating her tongue, Addison realised she presented a supremely humiliated sight for the woman to enjoy.

"You're quite right," Stern said, tucking his spent length back into his pants. "And take Addison down to the studio with you. She'll be co-hosting the show with you tonight."

Zoe stood up and strode to the door.

"When you've finished sucking cock and creaming yourself," Zoe said wearily, "join me in studio five." She scowled at Stern and said, "Send her down when she's ready."

Stern nodded and they both watched as Zoe flounced out of the office.

"Am I really getting a shot at working as a presenter?"

"For tonight."

When he saw her frown he added, "You'll get another shot tomorrow. If you excel in the challenges that I throw at you."

To her frustration, the inner muscles of her sex chose that moment to clench, reminding her that she was taking as much pleasure from receiving the humiliation as Stern was from giving it. Moving on unsteady legs, she started toward the door and then stopped.

"What am I expected to do on the radio show?"

He reached to his desk and retrieved a sheet of paper. Placing a kindly arm around her shoulder he walked with her down to studio five. The power in his muscular arms was a disquieting reminder of his desirable physique. The scents of citrus fruits and sandalwood that made up his cologne stirred another rush of need. He handed her the sheet of paper, and another clear bottle of mineral water and said, "Read that in your sexiest voice."

Then he sat outside the soundproof studio whilst Addison tried to make her sticky, wet backside comfortable on one of the studio's leather chairs.

"Eau Naturelle," Addison read. She put her lips closer to the microphone and lowered her voice to a breathy pout. "Eau Naturelle is the mineral water for when you need absolute satisfaction."

She took a swallow from the bottle and decided that was probably truer than most of the show's listeners would ever understand. Stern smiled and nodded and walked away leaving Addison alone in the studio with Zoe.

The brunette shook her head and regarded Addison with a sneer of distaste. She played a track, D.A.F. singing *Sex Unter Wasser*, and then muted the microphones so their conversation was private.

"Let me give you a word of advice," Zoe growled.

Addison considered her, not sure where this was going. Tony had described Zoe as a ball-breaker and Addison doubted the woman wanted to share her show with a newcomer. She guessed Zoe was going to tell her not to get comfortable in the co-host's chair and she steeled herself for the showdown.

Zoe took the clear bottle from Addison's hand.

She replaced it with a green bottle of mineral water.

"The green bottles are sparkling water. The clear bottles are still water and still water doesn't sparkle," Zoe explained. "If I was going to give you a word of advice, I'd say go with the sparkling. The next time Stern drenches your pussy, the sparkling bubbles add an extra thrill."

A DIVINE SOLUTION

◆◆◆◆

By

VINA GREEN

A Divine Solution

◆◆◆◆

Sarah lived in the biggest house on the highest hill. It had a red roof, and white gables, and was the only place in town that had remained relatively unaffected by the drought. No matter what the weather, the red house squatted on the hill, untouched.

Her husband, Tom, was the pastor. He was paid by the church and, as such, had no crops to worry about, nor cattle with nothing to eat and nowhere to graze.

She watched him now, through the big bay windows that looked out onto the vegetable patch where he had grown carrots, corn and runner beans, and beyond that the tall pines that stood erect in the distance, still solid and unmoving even after all that wind. Now it was a field of cracked earth. Nothing would grow until the rain came.

It was hot and humid, but he kept his shirt on, and all of the buttons fastened right up to the collar. Tom was a man of the cloth and not a labourer, but he believed that hard, physical work was a pathway to God. So he spent many hours outside, chopping wood or clearing stones from their large garden; and consequently his thick limbs strained against the seams of his shirt.

Sarah's thighs clenched involuntarily, and she turned away from the window.

They had only been married a year, but rarely made love. When they did, she always felt as though he was keeping a part of himself tethered back. Like a dog that bounds from it's cage, teeth snapping, only to be pulled back at the last moment by the taut strength of its leash.

She wished that he would let go, as he had only once, on their wedding night, even though everyone had hinted to her that few couples did 'it' on their wedding night.

Sarah hadn't known what to expect about anything. She had been a virgin until the day that she married.

Technically, it had not been their wedding night, as Tom hadn't waited for night to fall. He'd pulled over when they had driven only a half mile or so from the church and with his hands fluttering madly like sheets in a strong breeze he had lifted her white dress to her waist, leaned over the gear stick and buried his face between her legs, wetting her cunt with liberal strokes of his tongue before pushing her seat back, clambering across to lay overtop her body and piercing her through. By the time she realized what was coming he was inside her, and she felt a sharp stab that made her draw her breath, and then the wonderful sensation of being filled.

She hadn't wanted it to end, but it had, not even a minute after it had begun. He had suddenly collapsed on top of her and then awkwardly removed himself. His appendages were stiff, save for that part which mattered most to Sarah—his cock. Stiff as a wooden puppet, he manoeuvred himself back into the driver's seat, eased the car away from the kerb and drove them both to their new house: the red one on the hill.

She had lifted her skirts then. She wanted to look at herself, to see if she was different, now that she was no longer a virgin. To check if the hammering of her heart and the blissful headiness that had overtaken her brain were in any way reflected in her body. Slowly she drew the white silk up over her knees and then the pale expanse of her thighs. She spread her legs apart, tangled her fingers into the fabric and tugged her wedding dress all the way up to her waist.

She was wet, deliciously wet. Sarah could feel liquid dribbling from her pussy.

She watched as a droplet gathered, viscous and heavy as if one of the pearl buttons from her gown had been liquefied and transported to her cunt, and then rolled down her inner thigh before she lost sight of it.

There was no blood, and this fact excited Sarah. How such a thing were possible, she didn't know, as she had not so much as kissed a man before Tom. And yet here it was, the physical evidence that she was impure, a whore, a slut. He had taken her on the side of the road like a common animal.

Her mind was a maelstrom of thoughts and images, and as each flittered by she felt another stab of arousal through her middle, as though her mind was directly connected to her vagina.

A terrible thought—*no, she mustn't*—but she was a married woman now, so she rebelled against all of the things that she had learned about the way she ought to feel and behave as a single Christian woman.

Sarah took the tip of her finger and ran it between her slit, over the milk white offering that she knew was Tom's, the seed that he had left inside her. She brought it to her lips and sucked.

The flavour was tangy and acidic. Not comparable to anything that she had tasted before. A little like sweet water, but thicker, and with an edge of the sea.

She wondered if that was how holy water tasted, and blushed. What a wicked thought. Sarah giggled. A wild, ecstatic giggle, the sound of a woman who has torn away a part of herself only to find another part, so overwhelmingly different from the first that the realization made her hysterical with fear and excitement.

But Sarah's excitement was stronger than her fear.

Her finger was still in her mouth.

Tom, hearing this strange sound emitted from his new wife's lips; part wail and part whoop, glanced over.

His forearms were as stiff as lead pipes attached to the steering wheel. He had been so fixated on the mechanical act of driving the car—turn here, push down on the pedal, apply pressure to the gearstick—that he hadn't noticed Sarah lifting her skirts.

Now he saw her, naked from the waist down, legs spread, the geometric pattern of their mixed juices forming a map down her thighs, and her finger in her mouth.

He snatched it away.

"No more," he said. "No more."

Sarah pulled down her skirts and pressed her knees together. She clenched her legs harder and harder as they drove, imagining that the press of her muscles pushing against each other was the pressure of Tom's body moving inside her, but it was no use. She slumped back into the chair.

The gravel crunched as they pulled into the driveway. A soft sound that seemed far louder than it was when measured against the dull echo of silence that had gathered like a fog in the car.

Sarah opened the car door and pushed herself out. Tom was still fumbling with the keys. He did not pick her up and carry her over the threshold of their new home, as she had long imagined he would. He did not even hold her hand. He walked ahead of her with short, staccato steps, without looking back. She had to scurry to keep up and the sharp stones on the driveway bit into her feet. She was wearing flat silk slippers with thin soles, like ballet shoes, so that when they stood together at the ceremony everyone would see that he was taller than her, if only by an inch.

That was the way that it should be between a man and his wife.

"Your dress," he murmured, when they walked inside and she ran ahead of him, gasping with delight at the airy inside of the house that he had built for them with its wide, open expanses and the light that filtered in through the large bay windows. It was almost like living outside, with a roof.

She stopped. "My dress?"

"At the back. It needs to be washed." He reached forward and grasped the back of her skirt and she craned her neck around. There it was, a spot of blood, bright against the white background, the same coppery shade of red as the roof.

His jaw tightened. "It needs to be washed," he said again, and he pulled her across the wooden floor until they reached the bathroom.

It was a far larger bathroom than any that Sarah had seen before. The bath was set into the floor rather than standing on top of it, and it was more like a pool that could have comfortably fit four people, even six. It was surrounded by a slatted pine floor, sanded and polished to gleaming, pale wooden perfection.

Sarah removed her slippers before she tread on

it, an act of reverence. Tom walked quickly to the brass taps and turned them. The faucet itself was set into the wall, and protruded from it, hard and round and long and phallic. Steam filled the air, as soft and hushed as an exhalation of breath.

His face had taken on a paler than usual hue and his eyelids fluttered. His hands were tense and he flexed his fingers unconsciously as if were kneading dough. He was stripping his clothes off even as he strode back towards her and Sarah noticed that even the angles of his body had changed. His shoulders seemed more angular, the line of his limbs sharper. He cut through the air as he moved, his legs opening and closing like scissors.

The change in him made her pause. Sarah stood stock still in the moments that it took Tom to cross the room back to her, tearing at his cufflinks with violent haste. One came off into his hand easily, the other could not escape the tight prison of his shirt's buttonhole without a hard yank and the when the decorative jade green jewel finally came away from the silver claws that fixed it into place, it traced an arc through the growing fog of steam and landed with a clatter in the tub.

Tom had reached her now, and he grabbed her by the laces that held the bodice of her dress tight and dragged her backwards, turned her to face the bath and pushed her forwards.

"Get in," he said, just as she thought he was about

to push her over the porcelain lip of the tub and send her falling to her knees in the basin. His voice was rough like gravel, as deep as the plunge of a well. He had taken on the tone he used in his harsher sermons, when he was berating an unknown congregation for sins that had not yet been committed.

The offenses that caused the darkest shadows to fall across his brow were always sexual.

Before they married, Sarah had harboured a secret enjoyment of these talks. Watching his big hands clench and unclench, the rise and fall of his chest as his breathing became quicker, the orchestra of his arms drawing invisible crosses into the air as he spoke of the all the things she shouldn't do, shouldn't think about, shouldn't want to do. The dangers of masturbation and unnatural couplings between man and man or woman and woman, or those who favoured stimulating the anus, filling the entrance that could not lead to creation.

All the while Sarah would feel the hard wood of the pew pressing against her buttocks. She would spread her thighs a little beneath the modest barrier of her long skirt, flex her ankles, and imagine Tom forcefully dragging her behind the church wall to unceremoniously tug her skirt up and her underclothes down before pressing his cock into her asshole and fucking her hard until his hot seed flooded over the rise and fall of her buttocks.

Sometimes, afterwards, she would go home, rush

to her room and lie on her narrow, single bed with the smooth cream cover, and press her head into the pillow with her hand between her legs. She would rub herself and imagine him finding her like this and then punishing her by lifting her skirts and whipping her bare thighs.

She liked him best when he was angry.

They were part of a small, breakaway Christian sect, located in a tract of farmland in the rural American mid-West. Rules were strict and, among them, the notion that the practitioners should not socialize with unbelievers. So slowly, they had congregated to form a small community. Tom's father had been the pastor of the area and, with his death, Tom had been appointed to take over. Sarah's mother had converted when she had become pregnant with Sarah; and when her husband left her—walking out in the morning one day and never returning—she sought the church to provide her with support. Sarah had been born into it, and never known any differently.

Had she ever toyed with the idea of running away? Of leaving the community that she had been born to? Not really.

She hadn't thought much about it at all, besides the fact that she often felt as though she wasn't made for the rules she had to follow, or the rules weren't made for her. Sarah never dared to speak of the desire that filled her, or the images that regularly populated her daydreams or kept her awake at night.

Even stimulation as gentle as the flutter of long blades of grass caressing the soles of her feet, or the rush of a breeze against her bare arms, was enough to make Sarah slick between her thighs. Sex, and thoughts of sex, were her life blood, and the guilt that accompanied them like kerosene to a naked flame.

The keen longing that resulted from the repression of her sexual drive only made that drive grow stronger and stronger until it was like a demon that possessed her and allowed her to think of nothing else but cock and cunt and all of the ways that she wanted Tom, who now had the body of a strong brute of a man, yet retained the baby faced features of the boy that she had grown up with.

Her mind filled with perversions as she watched him standing atop of the church pulpit and lecturing valiantly on all the things Sarah shouldn't do, his eyes glittering all the while like sunbeams bouncing off pools of cool clear water.

He didn't pay the slightest attention to Sarah, or anyone else for that matter, until she asked to be baptised.

One of the points of theology that separated their group from many other Christian churches was the practice of adult baptism. Sarah had seen Tom perform a baptism the previous summer. She remembered the vision of him standing in the wide river that ran near the churchyard, the water lapping all the way to his chest, his white shirt soaked through and sticking to his body, revealing the faint hint of his small hard nipples. The look on his face as he had taken the younger man being baptised into his arms and dunked him under. Held him there a fraction too long for comfort, it was thought, as Timothy emerged what felt like a long while later, water streaming from his nose, heroically trying to stifle a cough.

Tom had risen from the water and strode straight back to the white washed wooden church, ducking through the door without saying a single word to anyone. Sarah watched him as he walked. The trousers he wore for the baptism were also white, though of thicker material than his cotton shirt, so not so sheer when wet. The material clung to him, revealing the round hills of his ass, the muscled shape of his thighs. He disappeared inside and did not return for almost half an hour. Getting dry, they all supposed, and nothing was said of it although everyone thought it strange that he would leave the newly baptised Timothy to pull himself from the stream and formally greet his new congregation alone.

When it was Sarah's turn, she didn't even notice the coldness of the water. Within a few steps from the bank it was as deep as her underarms. Her nipples were hard, and she knew that despite what others might think, that was not the result of the temperature. Tom's hands were on her waist, holding her steady, but then they slipped down to each side of her hips, scooting nearer than she knew was modest to the curve of her buttocks.

She crossed her arms over her breast and leaned back against him as he prepared to lower her into the water for what was traditionally a quick dunk. She hoped it would be longer. A hawk cut a dark line through the bright blue sky overhead and then Sarah closed her eyes, Tom tipped her back, and water flooded over her face.

Seconds passed. Three, and then five, six, seven. She began to feel giddy. Then she felt one of his long arms reach between her legs and his hand clasp the hem of her dress and pull it upwards and as quick as a fish jumping onto a hook his fingers were inside her, pumping, once, twice, three times and the blissful shock of it nearly caused Sarah to gasp and breathe a mouthful of water into her lungs.

Just as she thought she might pass out, he pulled her skirt down again and pushed her to the surface and he was gone, striding out of the water and towards the church, leaving her swaying on her feet in the river, alone.

Her mother, and others in the congregation commented that it had been a beautiful thing to see. That her face when she surfaced was radiant. That she looked as though she had had a communion with God.

He did not speak to her for weeks afterwards. Then, suddenly, out of the blue, he asked her mother for permission to court her, and after just a fortnight of chaperoned early dinners and one dance that took place with their arms outstretched, Tom proposed marriage.

Their engagement, too, was rushed. They married within four months, just long enough for Tom to finish the house that he was building on the hill.

That first night, just after she had tentatively stepped into the bathtub under his instruction, she thought of the baptism, and it occurred to her that Tom was aroused by water.

The tub was so deep—much deeper than an ordinary bath—she'd had to carefully tuck her full skirt beneath her and perch on the edge and then lower herself in. He had bent down and placed one hand on the edge and jumped, so close he was nearly on top of her. His impatience was palpable, and almost anger. Though there was no malice in it, nor any real temper or frustration. No, the emotion wasn't quite anger. It was longing. Sarah recognized that feeling as easily as she knew her own shadow, for it had followed her for as long as she could remember.

This time, instead of pulling her into the water he put his hand on the back of her head and pushed her forward. She plunged in, face first, spluttering until he pulled her out again and let her catch her breath. Then he pushed her towards the opposite lip so that she could steady herself on the edge of the pool as he lifted her skirts up and prepared to enter her from behind. Her petticoats spread out on the surface like a parachute, and he bundled a bunch up on either side and pushed the fabric into her hands, indicating that she should keep it lifted for him.

Although the bath was deep it had only filled enough to reach the back of her thighs when she was standing. He curved his palms through the water, creating a pair of waves that rippled across the surface and then up and over her buttocks in a wet slap. He cupped his hands and threw scoops over her back. Rivulets poured over her shoulders, following the curve of her breasts that hung in front of her as she bent over like the udders of a cow, and formed droplets on the pointed nubs of her nipples. She felt a current of air, cool after the sting of the hot water, and then the wet smack of his hand as he brought his palm down first on one ass cheek, and then the other. She hissed from the shock of it, and gripped the lip of the tub tighter to avoid losing her balance. He ran the blade of his hand between the valley of her ass, the hard points of his fingers pressing against her asshole.

They developed a rhythm between them. As the pressure of his fingertips against her hole became more insistent, she pushed back against him, and he thrust further forward, until the push and pull of their desire was like the pulsing tide of the sea. A silent conversation of want, each of them intimating that with this new and forbidden exploration, they were fulfilling the need of the other and not their own desire. His fingers were inside her now, and as she relaxed and allowed him to enter he pushed deeper and began to thrust.

She moaned, a sound that was something like a croak. Despite the humidity in the air, her throat felt as dusty dry as the fields around them would soon become, as dry as a sand dune in the midday sun. She licked her lips, trying to moisten them but it was no use, as if all of the moisture in her body had been drawn down to her vagina. She was seeping, sodden. Wetness dripped from the folds of her cunt into the water below her.

Sarah steadied herself with one hand and reached the other between her legs. She grazed her clit and the unexpected touch, after so much longing, swept through her in one sharp jolt as though she had been irradiated. But it was not her clit that she was seeking. She fumbled at the air, reached the strong bulk of Tom's thigh and travelled higher until she brushed against the softness of his balls, and then the hard pole of his cock. The effort nearly unbalanced her but she clung to the slippery edge of the tub as she wrapped her fingers around the base of his shaft and tried to angle the path of his erection towards her cunt. She wanted him inside her, but he resisted her touch, and batted her hand away. He caught her as she nearly slipped sideways and lowered her hand back onto the bath's edge.

His torso curved over her back and his penis jutted, a rigid point that jabbed against her leg until he stood upright again and directed it between her buttocks. Sarah raised her rump a little, using her body to nudge him lower, towards the entrance of her pussy but Tom was insistent.

He dragged his cock up and down, following the same path that he had caressed with the flat of his hand earlier. When his cock head found the dip of her anus he let it rest there for a few moments and then began to gently push, to ease her open. Her hands turned white as she gripped the tub tighter in anticipation of what would come next.

Thoughts flickered in her mind, darting in and out of her consciousness like seabirds skimming the surface of the ocean but never settling. Her mind warred with her body. One thinking, questioning; would it hurt? Would God punish her for sodomy? Did she want this?

Her flesh paid no attention to her thoughts and simply processed these new sensations; the way the silky velvet tip of his cock head felt pressing against her asshole, the sound of his breathing, increasingly laboured, the warmth of his saliva as he pulled away for a moment, spat on her and used his fingers to work the lubricant into her hole. He repeated this process again and again until she was wet and relaxed enough for him to slide inside. Just an inch, at first. He held still, and she held her breath. She exhaled and relaxed a little more and he slid a little further inside her. Eventually, the full length of his shaft was buried inside her ass, and she was rocking back and forward against him, pushing her rear up against his groin, encouraging him to thrust deeper and deeper. He was holding onto her hips now, one hand on either side of her buttocks. His thrusts becoming faster, more urgent.

Sarah did not want him to go limp again and leave her empty and aching for more, as he had in the car earlier. She scooted her left arm across in front of her to centre her body and with her right hand she delved between her folds. A soft hiss escaped her lips, the sound of an out breath through her teeth at the sheer relief she took in pleasuring herself. Tom hadn't even noticed. He was kneading her buttocks in his hands, pulling away and half slapping her in his effort to hold her hips in place as his pumping became more frenzied.

Sarah found her rhythm, quick circular strokes over her nub, occasionally dipping into her well to wet her fingertips before sliding through her furrow again and applying just the right degree of pressure to her clitoris, the peculiar physics of self love.

But she was too late, or too slow, or rather, Tom was too quick. He lasted far longer than he had the first time, perhaps because it was his second release in a few hours, or maybe because the circumstances were less hurried. When he came, he collapsed against her and she fell forward. Instinctively, she drew her right hand away from it's position between her thighs and threw it out in front of her to catch her balance.

The ache of her frustration was a sharp knife twist, rapid and cutting. His cock softened and flopped out of her as he pulled away.

He stepped out of the tub and the water rippled

and splashed around her.

She didn't turn to look at him.

"Dry yourself," he said, "and come to bed." She heard the soft whump of a towel hitting the wooden floorboards nearby.

After their wedding night, Tom could barely bring himself to touch Sarah. When they made love, which happened rarely, he would simply roll on top of her, spend his seed, and roll away.

Sometimes as she was dressing, she felt his eyes on her, drinking her in as though she were the only pool of water in a desert, but when she glanced back at him, he turned his head away. They lay next to each other in bed at night as stiff as boards, and she felt as though her limbs were frozen in place by her sides. She wanted to reach over and touch him but there was an insurmountable wall between them that even the full strength of her lust could not breach.

Sarah stopped touching herself. The weight of Tom's disapproval was too great. She felt as though he had turned her hands to lead. She found no outlet for it, nor respite from it, but her desire never waned.

Then the drought started. At first, it was just a dry spell, an Indian summer, an absence of rain. But gradually the things that grew on the land around them began to droop and wither. Then the ground began to crack in places as though it was tearing away from itself. Even the air felt parched, and the wind that blew clouds of dust up in flurries carried with it a faint metallic aroma, a scent of death and decay. It was as though the earth had a thirst that could never be quenched, and knew it.

Finally, the river that ran around the church dried up. At first, it just shrank away a little from the edges, but before long, what had once been a clean, wide ribbon, clear as glass and swift as quicksilver flowing across the land turned the colour of an old leather shoe and stopped moving. For a while, it took on the appearance of a dirty wound cutting through the fields, like a deep scratch from a rusty blade that refused to heal.

Twice, she heard water running—a sound that was unmistakable now, since everyone's ears keened to hear that steady rush—and filling a bath to bathe was prohibited, since the reservoirs were so low. She crept down the stairs and padded softly to the bathroom and listened. Mingled with the sound of the flowing tap she heard Tom's soft, desperate moans, and a steady, moist slap, slap, slap; the sound of a pot of thick porridge on a heavy, rolling boil. It was a noise she hadn't heard before and yet instinctively she knew what it was. It was a sound that made her feel like a voyeur. Her eyes widened, and she smoothed her hair back from her face and hurried away, padding quickly towards the kitchen on the soft naked soles of her feet.

Tom preached fervently about how the dry soil reflected the community's lack of spiritual richness. That the rain would come when they repented and God forgave their sins. They were all at fault, he said, in that voice of his that boomed like thunder, but Sarah felt as though he was speaking only to her. *This is your fault*, his voice seemed to say, for wanting more. For wanting, always. For she felt as empty and wanting as the land was dry, her desire as strong as the rush of a waterfall and twice as deep as the deepest ocean.

And while the sun baked everything else in it's path, Sarah was about the only thing in town that did not take on the appearance of clay that's spent too long in a potter's kiln.

She was luminous, in a pale pink dress, the colour of cotton candy, with the flush that always coloured her cheeks, her eyes big, round and long-lashed like a doe, and her hair as thick and blonde and bouncing as it had been when she was a toddler. Her skin was quite fair and she did not tan, no matter how long she spent outdoors. Although her preference for a large brimmed straw hat with a wide ribbon that tied around her narrow chin, long skirts and a light shawl to cover her arms, meant that it was rare for her skin to see the sun.

Her breasts had grown so full that they ached, and the dresses and blouses that had previously sat loose and modest over her chest now visibly struggled to restrain the weight of her bosom. Her nipples were permanently hard, and formed stiff nubbins, apparent through the cloth that covered them. The natural pallor of her skin, which in her childhood had drawn suggestions of anaemia and marked her out as different from the other children who ran over fields in the afternoon and returned brown as Indians, now took on the strength of marble, the glow of a full moon in a cloudless sky. The wetness that seeped between Sarah's legs in a constant flow now permeated her whole being. She was like a white skinned, over ripe plum. Given one gentle caress she would burst, and rain her thick juices over everything in her path.

She attracted glances as she walked through town and sat listening to Tom's sermons. From men—and more than a few women—who, by the look in their eyes, craved to be near her, to soak up some of the moisture that radiated from her into the air. The gossip moved in turns. At first, they referred to her as a blushing bride. Then it was rumoured that perhaps she bore a child. But as time passed and her belly retained its flatness, the current of gossip became quieter and more severe. Whispers moved in eddies, pooling in dark places.

Sarah observed the idle chatter between the older women. Some of them had taken to wearing headscarves, folded triangles of brightly coloured cloth perched on the tops of the heads so they resembled aging birds, like squat owls with one contrary bright plumage. They did not speak to her anymore.

She had travelled to the end of that long road now,

from an innocence and youthful enthusiasm that they could pet and mould to womanhood, but it was apparent that on reaching the end of that journey she had not become one of them. They stared at her with bright raisin eyes and thin lips and did not say a word. But the horror of their disapproval, all the things that remained unspoken, hung over her like a cloud. She spent more and more time alone.

She had nothing to do besides cook and clean, for that was the way of things. Without water, or with very little of it, cleaning became harder, and took longer. As the pastor's wife, Tom said, it was up to her to set an example. So, even though nobody else was there to see her, she did not use a mop and bucket to clean the floors but rather she got down on her knees with a small brush and scrubbed, sometimes using spit to moisten the dust, or the juice of a lemon. She polished the wooden floors with a soft cloth and a few spoonfuls of vegetable oil.

It was a hot day in July, and Sarah was on all fours scrubbing the wide expanse of their open kitchen and dining room. She was in the centre of the floor with her skirts spread around her like a child's ballerina toy. Beams of morning sun filtered through the tall glass windows and sent lines of light flooding across the room, interspersed with darker beams of shadow, trapping her in the centre like a canary in a dappled cage. She wore the lemon yellow dress that had once been her favourite for church, but was now relegated to home use only, since her breasts now spilled overtop of the bodice. Before she married, the shade—and few could wear it—had simply suited her. Now, with its thick rope of white embroidered edging, and the peculiar gleam of her skin, it gave her the look of a lemon meringue pie. Sweet and soft and lush, inviting a hungry mouth to take a bite of her moist flesh.

The floorboards that felt so smooth when she walked across them barefoot took on the texture of concrete beneath her knees. She had come across a darker fleck of unidentifiable grime that could not be shifted. Perhaps it was a fleck of burned food, or soil that had found it's way inside, although Tom was fastidious about brushing off his clothes and shoes before he set foot in the house. She stopped, leaned back on her hind and drew her hand across her brow in a gesture that spoke of resignation, although she had not yet given up. Then, emboldened by the brief pause she spread her legs further apart to steady her centre of gravity, leaned forward and scrubbed harder, putting so much of her body weight into each stroke of the brush that her arm and shoulder moved back and forth like a piston.

Through it all she was aware of the moisture that gathered between her thighs, as it always did. She no longer wore undergarments, unless she was out in public. They were just more clothes to wash, and they didn't have the water for that. With her legs spread like they were, and her body hinging back and forward she had raised a gentle breeze that brushed against her bare cunt, like the gentle pads of invisible fingers stroking her softly.

One patch of floor complete, she scooted back, revealing the square of flooring that she had been kneeling over. A pool of fluid had gathered there. Sarah placed her palms on either side, bowed her head down like a dog and sniffed it, then lapped a little up on her tongue. The liquid was slightly more viscous than water, but not as thick as oil. It was almost, but not quite odourless. The only one other time that she had tasted her juices, they had been mixed with Tom's, and carried the metallic, sea salt tang of oysters, and a slight quinine bitterness. Her fluid alone had a faint aroma that she could not relate to anything else. It made her think of the earth. Cloying, damp soil, thick with life. A place of darkness and light, like the odour that might emanate from the thickest, most impenetrable jungle, the scent of things growing. The taste was mild and sweet. She could have drunk a cup of it, and felt her thirst quenched forever.

Sarah bowed her head again, still supporting her body with the palms of her hands, so from above, her shoulders knotted, folding in on themselves like an angel without wings, like a pilgrim prostrating in prayer. She drank from the spring of her own fount, and when she was done, she rose up and walked outside. There, she stood on a patch of cracked dry soil, spread her legs, and let the wetness that continued to spread from her cunt rain down over what was left of her herb garden.

She had grown chervil here, lacy lime green bushes that stood two feet tall at least and spread in thick, cloudy bushes like a forest of carrot tops that she couldn't cut back quick enough, no matter how many salads she garnished. She'd cut bunches of it, tied them with twine and taken them to church, the smell of aniseed lingering on her palms long after she had given the posies away. There had been rosemary here too, a whole shrub of it, and sprawling patches of mint and thyme. Now, what was left of the herb garden resembled the burning bush that had troubled Moses, after the flame had passed through it. The earth was cracked underfoot and where the remnants of plants lay there were either brown sticks that crumbled into dust with the slightest pressure or a tangle of withered, soft brown stems, too fragile to hold up even the weight of the dead leaves they still carried.

Droplet upon droplet pearled down from her and soaked into the earth below. She stood there and enacted this private rainstorm until the bright orange yolk of the sun began to disappear behind the pines that ran along the skyline around the house and she heard the crunch of tires on driveway gravel as the car turned in with Tom at the wheel.

Sarah gathered her skirts and ran inside, before he saw her and asked what she was doing. She needn't have worried. Tom was so caught up in himself that he didn't even notice that she had only half finished the floors and hadn't started dinner. Sarah reheated soup, made from their store of root vegetables, mixed with grains, and fried pieces of yesterday's bread in dripping. Tom went straight upstairs to change out of his stiffly starched suit and wipe the dust from his face. As she filled his bowl, she had the urge to spit into it, but she didn't. By the time he returned, ready to eat, she had set the table with a linen cloth and put away the brushes that she had been using to clean the floor. She didn't have time to change out of the yellow dress. He sat down, pulled his chair close to the table and glanced at her, his eyes automatically focusing on the wide expanse of her cleavage. He blinked, and looked away.

"How were they today?" she asked him.

Tom had been out proselytising to the communities around them, blaming the weather and the subsequent failure of the crops on their lack of faith. Some folk listened. He was an engaging speaker. Some believed. Others told him to get the hell out, and he moved on nonplussed to the next location and tried again.

"The Earth is full of lawlessness," he replied, quoting from Genesis. He held a hunk of fried bread in both hands and tore chunks from it with his teeth so fiercely that his head lashed from side to side as he pulled back between bites. Sarah shrunk back into her seat. Then she thought of her herb garden, moistened with the fluid of her desires, and straightened her back. That earth, she thought, was full of lawlessness. Lawlessness, lasciviousness, licentiousness, libidinous lust. She brought her spoon to her lips and swallowed.

That night she was not plagued by violent dreams,

nor by the ache in her loins that caused her to lie awake long after Tom started snoring, a soft wheezing sound, akin to an old man's death rattle. When she did sleep, she slept the long torpor of the untroubled, and awoke to the sound of Tom's startled cry, and the clatter of his footsteps taking the stairs to their bedroom two at a time.

His voice was joyful.

"Sarah! Sarah!" he cried. The door flung open as he pushed it so hard it hit the wall behind with a bang. It was the first time that he had called her by name in as long as she could remember.

"Get up," he said, and he pulled her by the hand, down the stairs and out the door, not even stopping to insist that she pull on a robe to cover her nightgown. "Look!" he shouted, pointing downwards in the manner of a prophet delivering a curse. His forefinger jutting taut, his fist clenched, his whole arm shaking. The subject of his gaze was Sarah's herb garden. What had, the previous afternoon, been a dry patch of withered sticks had blossomed overnight. The soil was dark and moist, and punctuated by new green shoots that had sprung to the surface, seeking light. Tom fell to his knees, cupped his hands together and lifted a scoop of the damp loam up, holding it aloft like an offering to the heavens. He began to pray.

"A miracle," he muttered. "We have been blessed."

He ran to the water tank at the back of the property.

They collected their own water, as well as using the town reservoir supply, but it had not rained in months and the tank had long been dry. He heaved the hinged covering up and held it there for a few moments, then lowered it down again with the reverence of an undertaker closing a casket.

He turned to face her. His face had turned deathly pale.

"It's full," he said. "The tank is full."

"But it hasn't rained?" she replied.

"Silly woman," he said to her, "lacking faith, even after this." His hands gesticulated wildly. "Are you so blind that you cannot see? This is the work of God. A message from God."

Word spread through the town and the towns around them and people came to see for themselves the miracle of the garden that grew in the drought and the tank that filled with rain when the skies had been wrung out for months. Their neighbours came from far away with buckets and begged to be allowed to fill a pail and take it home. They blessed Tom and Sarah to their faces, but chattered like a flock of magpies behind their backs about the charismatic pastor, his pale, beautiful wife and the miracle that had occurred, but only for the benefit of the red-roofed house on the hill.

The matrons called it witchcraft, and they blamed Sarah, and refused to use the water.

"It's driven my husband mad," they whispered to

one another, and shared stories of men who'd taken one sip of the miracle water with its earthen tang and lost their minds. Women who drank it appeared more youthful. Their smiles were broader and their frowns disappeared. They abandoned the stiffness of their petticoats and let the curve of their hips sway as they walked.

But most called it an act of God, proof that He could cause the rain to fall and the crops to grow again if they served Him right. Tom's sermons drew larger and larger crowds as religious folk from the communities around them abandoned their own churches in favour of the man who could give them water. They called him the new Messiah, and they filled all of the pews, lined the sides of the walls, and even stood outside, listening through the windows.

Tom began to undertake baptisms at home, in the bathtub. He baptised new followers, and he encouraged older converts to renew their vows of faith and be drenched again in God's water. The river water that they had been baptised in was unclean, he said, and the drought was a sign from God that their sins had not been washed away. Now God had given them water, a sign that they should use it to wash their sins away again.

He undertook these rituals privately. Even the individual's family were not permitted to watch.

"The moment you offer yourself to God," he said, "should be a private affair, not one witnessed by a herd of curious onlookers watching as though they're at the cinema."

"Double dunking," muttered some of the older members of the church, those who had known Tom's father. But they came to him anyway, because everything seemed strange these days and what else did they have to put their faith in?

And so it was that instead of gathering on what had been a blanket of grass in front of the church steps by the river and was now a cracked, dusty platform of baked earth, the congregation gathered in town, at the foot of the hill and looked up at the red-roofed house waiting for Pastor Tom to bring down the newest member of their faith, or an existing member, renewed.

Yet when they appeared, the faces of the converts were not flushed with the innocence of the sinner reborn. They bore a different kind of glow. The glow of the desirous, the steady, radiant light that thrums from the hearts of those who have discovered longing and welcomed it. They were a people who had quenched one thirst and replaced it with another, a thirst for earthly things.

Those who had been baptised in this new water stopped going to church. At first they tried to explain it when they were asked why they had lost their faith.

"Because I'd rather feel the sun on my face," one said.

"God exists in the stars," said another.

But the words sounded hollow even to their own ears so before long, they just ignored the question.

They hungered for the elements. For the breath of wind on their skin and the moisture of rain on their hair, the sweetness of a strawberry bursting between full lips. They hungered for each other. Husbands kissed their wives in the streets, and they kissed other wives' husbands.

Even Tom began to change. He ignored the complaints of the steadfast parishioners who came to him and said that Sarah was a she-devil and this fountain that had appeared in his yard was cursing the congregation, turning them all into sinners.

"Drink," he said, and he filled them a glass. "Let all ye who are thirsty come, and drink from the fountain of the river of life."

They accused him of misusing scripture and he ignored them, and gulped the contents of the glass down himself.

She found him, one afternoon, naked and swimming in the rainwater tank. He wore the unknowing, untroubled expression of a child, simply glorying in the joy of being wet.

But all of this was not enough for Sarah. She wanted the river to return and for blankets of grass to cover the fields, for the ground to crack open and spout geysers of hot mud.

She woke Tom in the night. Or at least, she woke

his cock. Whether or not he thought the rest of it was a dream, she wasn't sure. As soon as he was stiff, she slid onto his shaft, and she rode him with all of the energy of a woman possessed. She took hold of his hands and placed them upon her breasts and she held onto his hips and drove her mound against his groin so that his flesh repeatedly grazed her clitoris. Faster and faster she rocked, and outside, the wind began to rise in gusts that rattled the windowpanes, and rain began to fall.

When she came, her cunt ran a river over his shaft. She collapsed on top of him, spent, at last, rolled away, and fell asleep.

The next day, she got out of bed and put her yellow dress on and took the car keys and drove. The gravel crunched, but this time she didn't hear it, because the sound of streams rushing was everywhere. Rain still fell, but in most places, the earth was so dry and cracked that the water seemed to just spill over, as though the dirt were oil.

It took a while for the moisture to seep back into the ground, for the mud to come, for things to grow again in the way that they always had.

But grow they did, and so did she, far away from the town where the river now ran again, bubbling through the long grass as though it had never been dry.